Contents

Thug Paradise

Mz. Lady P

Literary Queen Publications

Chapter 1 - King Carter

Young Rich Nigga

Ever since Thug gave his position to me, business has been good and the money is flowing abundantly. My crew and I are bringing in more money in a week than most niggas bring home in a lifetime. Thug told me five years ago my life would change for the better. All I needed to do was get on his team and assemble my crew. At the age of sixteen, my little brother Nasir, our best friend Dutch, and I were known around the hood as the Jack Boys. We robbed any motherfucking body we wanted. We bodied any nigga that refused. That's what put us on Thug's radar. Thug wanted us on his team but we couldn't do anymore robberies. We would sell for him and do hits with him and his crew. Since that day five years ago when he approached us, our lives have drastically changed for the better. He upheld his end of the bargain and we upheld ours.

I'm thankful that we linked up with Thug. He isn't just our Boss. He's like a father figure. We didn't really have any family so when we were introduced to his family, they became the closest thing we had to a family. Growing up I wished we had a family like theirs. Momma Peaches goes so hard for them. The only thing our mother went hard for was a crack pipe. We've never met our father. Our grandmother said that our father could be any man in the city of Chicago because our mother was a prostitute.

Our grandmother wasn't shit either. She didn't pass up a chance to belittle or ridicule us because of our mother's fuck ups. We didn't stand a chance when Trixie abandoned us. She literally walked out the door without as much as a goodbye. I was twelve and Nasir was eleven. My grandmother didn't want anything to do with us so we were on our own. That's when the robbing and killing started. We had to do whatever we had to in order to survive. I would roll over and die fifty times before I let us go hungry.

Our grandmother got wind of what we were doing and reported us to the authorities. When the Department of Children and Family Services caught up with us, we were placed into the foster care system. I thank God every day for them not separating us.

We kept running away from our foster homes so we were sent to the Juvenile Detention Center. That's where we met Dutch. The three of us together were nothing nice on the inside. We ran our housing unit with an iron fist. We were taking niggas dinner trays and making them pay us to keep from getting their asses beat. It was either get down or lay down when we were involved.

After a couple of months of being locked up, the state convinced our grandmother to take custody of us. She didn't give a fuck as long as she got her check and her cut from our robberies. We didn't get any complaints from her. I made enough money to pay her off and she took Dutch in as well. His mother wanted nothing to do with him so she turned over her parental rights. It was on and popping then. It's been us against the world ever since. She died about two years after taking us in and I have never been so happy about seeing someone lowered into the ground.

Now, at the age of twenty-two, I have more money than I know what to do with. Living the lavish lifestyle has never felt better. It feels good to give my baby girl, Imani, whatever her heart desires. She's only two but I spoil her and her mother, Gucci, rotten.

I've been fucking with Gucci since I was sixteen years old .She's been around through everything and has never once left a nigga. I'm surprised she's been around this long, especially since we're not exclusive. She has my heart in her pocket but I mess around with other bitches from time to time. It's not that I don't love her. I'm just not ready to settle down and put my all into a relationship. She's free to have with other niggas. She chooses not to. That's how much she loves a nigga. Plus, she know ain't no nigga gon' lay this pipe to her like I do or spend this bread on her like me.

Yeah, I'm a young rich nigga with a cocky attitude. I came from nothing and worked my way up in the streets. I proved myself to one of the most ruthless get money ass niggas the streets of the Chi had ever seen. Thug doesn't trust just anyone with his legacy so I know that I have to stay on my shit and run these streets with an iron fist just like he has.

****

"What's up Boss Lady?" I asked Tahari as I walked inside their home for my weekly meeting with Thug.

"Nothing. I'm just trying to get this anniversary party ready and my husband doesn't want to give me any more money." Tahari spoke loudly so that Thug could hear her.

"You don't need any more money. You've already spent over fifty thousand dollars. That's too much for a party Ta-Baby. I'm not giving you nothing else so don't ask any more," Thug said as he walked into the foyer and we dapped each other up. I couldn't do shit but laugh at them.

"It's the one year anniversary of Thug Inc. We have to go all out, Ka'Jaire. Please let me spend some more money. I'll use my shop money. I just want this party to be epic. They will be talking about this party years from now." She walked over and whispered something in his ear. The look on his face let me know he was about to give in.

"Twenty thousand. That's it, nothing more." Tahari walked off smiling and winked at me.

"I see who wear the pants around here." We both laughed.

"Hell yeah. My wife is wicked with a gun. Trust me; you don't want to get on her bad side. Come on let's go in my office and talk business."

We walked back to his office and got right down to business. I handed him a duffle bag with ten million dollars inside. It was his payout for the month.

"I'm impressed. When I was your age, I was probably only bringing in five million a month. Keep up the good work. I see that the cash flow is good. Is there anything else going on in the streets I should be aware of?" he asked as he thumbed through the stacks of money.

"Nothing major. I got Dutch and Nasir on this lil nigga Rocko. I heard he's been on some greasy shit lately. Talking out the side of his neck in regard to Thug Inc and our west side traps. They haven't been able to catch up with him, but as soon as I do, I'm going to cut his fucking tongue out and mail it to his mother."

"Yeah. Dead that nigga immediately. Loose lips sink ships," Thug said as he handed me one million back.

"What's this for, Boss?"

"That's for you and Gucci. Take her on a trip and do something nice for her. I'll let Nasir run things until you get back. I won't take no for an answer. Make sure you get fitted for your tux. My wife insists that the party be a black tie affair. No gym shoes. Let the whole team know that if they come with gym shoes on my wife will not hesitate to put their asses out.

"I got you." We did the Thug Inc handshake and I was out.

I hadn't seen Gucci or my daughter in two days. I knew Gucci was about to be wilding. I made sure to be high as a kite. That nagging was about to give me a migraine. I had every intention on drowning her ass out. If she went overboard, I would get up and leave.

That's another thing about our relationship. We live in two separate houses. It's better for me that way. I know that Gucci wants us to live together, but I like my personal space. One day, I'll take that leap and make things official with Gucci. She's a good girl and she deserves it. Plus, she's the only female that can melt this ice around my heart. My mother really messed a nigga up in the head. Gucci says that I have issues with my mother and that's why I can't commit. I really don't know what it is. I'm confused about the shit myself. The only thing I'm sure of is getting this bread and making sure my seed and my bitch are straight. Everything else is irrelevant.

I pulled into Gucci's parking space and noticed her car was gone. I was glad as hell. I could go to sleep and feel her wrath later. I parked and went inside her house through the side door. I almost stepped back out because I thought I was in the wrong crib. The condo was completely empty. I went from room to room checking to see where her and my daughter were at. It looked like no one had ever lived there. I picked up the phone to call her and the line was disconnected. I punched a hole in the wall. I couldn't believe Gucci just up and left. This bitch took my daughter. I guess she was telling the truth when she told me that one day I was going to look up and my family would be gone.

Chapter 2 - Gucci Lennox
Treat Me Like Somebody

I love King. Lords knows I do, but I can't deal with the bullshit anymore. I've tried my best to be patient with him and let him conquer the streets. However, I'm tired of being last on his list. Our daughter and I should come before this street shit. Don't get me wrong, my baby is a hustler to his heart. I don't knock him for his ambition, but there's more to life than that.

The worst thing I could have ever done was be comfortable with us not being exclusive or living together. Since I was sixteen years old, all I wanted was to be a part of King's world. As long as we spent time together, I was cool. Even if it meant sharing him with random bitches. Things are different now. We're older and we're parents.

Imani deserves her mommy and daddy living in the same house. It's been nothing but broken promise after promise. I love King with all my heart, but I'm tired of playing the fool for his ass. He thinks everything is cool as long as he keeps me laced in the finest clothing and luxury vehicles. I love that he gives me the world without me asking for it. However, those materialistic things don't keep me warm or sexually satisfied at night.

Leaving King is the hardest thing that I ever had to do, but I had to do it. I need to show him that I'm not some kept bitch that he can play games with. King got me twisted if he thinks he can keep playing with my heart like this. I'd rather sleep alone every night than lay in bed with a broken heart. I've been more than a ride or die chick, woman, and friend to him. I was there when he drove a broke down Chevy. I need to get on my grown woman shit. King got me fucked all the way up if he thinks he will continue to have his cake and eat it too.

King's newfound street status along with his looks has bitches flocking to him. King is so sexy. He's tall and cocky with shoulder length dreads that he keeps maintained. His light brown skin and brown eyes are enough to have any woman wanting to fuck him on sight. I always tell him that he's pretty. He hates when I say that. It's the truth though. He knows it too he just doesn't want to admit it. He is so cocky and confident. That's what I liked about him when we first met. He let it be known these niggas didn't have shit on him. My baby was one of kind and that's what made me fall in love him. Not to mention the dick lashing he gives me. There is no better feeling than his massive dick filling me up.

As I drove over to my new apartment in Maywood, Illinois, I felt bad about not telling my mother where I was moving. I had no choice though. She would rat me out to King in a second. She loved him because he reminded her of my father, Sincere Lennox. He was known as "Ox" on the streets of the Chi.

Back in the day, he was a vicious and notorious pimp. My mother was his bottom bitch. My sisters, Dior and Chanel, and I are the offspring of a pimp and his hoe. I loved my mom though. She went through hell and high water to make sure we had the finer things in life after my father was killed in a drug deal gone bad. She claimed she had a night job. We weren't fools. She was out selling pussy, but I would never judge her. She did what she had to do.

King can do no wrong in my mother's eyes and that really hurts me because I need her support. Thank God that I have my sisters. I can tell them anything, but I'm skeptical to tell them where I am. Dior is with Dutch and Chanel is in a relationship with Nasir. Chanel won't say nothing to Nasir, but Dior can't hold hot water when it comes to Dutch. Dutch definitely wears the pants in their relationship. He is not working with a full deck. I'm the oldest, Dior is the middle child, and Chanel is the baby. She's the craziest of us all. She and Nasir fight like cats and dogs. However, I love Dutch and Nasir. They are the brothers I never had.

****

After two weeks of being M.I.A. I started to feel bad for my daughter. She was missing her Daddy and I going crazy in the house. The walls of my new apartment were starting to close in on me. It was imperative that I get some fresh air. I know that my mother is probably going crazy looking for me. I decided not to call first. I just popped up on her doorstep.

"Get your ass in here right now! Do you know how crazy we have all been going looking for you?" my mother said as she grabbed Imani out of my arms and kissed all over her face.

"I'm sorry, Mommy. I just needed to get away that's all." I held my head down as I spoke to her because I knew her lecture would come next.

"King has been wreaking havoc on the city looking for you. I'm about to call him and your sisters to let them know that you're okay."

"No! Don't tell King I'm here. You can call Dior and Chanel, that's it." I grabbed her cell phone from her hand letting her know I was serious.

"I know you have lost your fucking mind grabbing my phone out of my hand. Since when you started disrespecting me, Gucci?"

"I'm not trying to disrespect you, Mommy. I'm asking you not to call King." I couldn't help the tears that were falling.

"Don't cry, Gucci. I won't call him but you can't just up and leave your relationship when things get bad. It's not about you and King. Imani is what's important."

She walked away with my daughter. I fell back on the couch because I knew my mother was about to call King at that very moment. Something inside of me said not to come over here. I should have followed my first mind. I thought about leaving. Instead, I stayed and got ready for World War III.

I pulled my hair up in a ponytail because I knew we were about to come to blows. I didn't give a fuck what happened. I wasn't bowing down to King anymore. I was surprised because King didn't show up. I headed home alone for the first time. My mother wanted Imani to stay with her for the night. I was hesitant because I didn't want King to come and take her. I couldn't refuse my mother her granddaughter so I let her stay.

I was tired so tired when I made it home. All I wanted to do was take a shower, eat something, and go to sleep. The feeling of someone's hand covering my mouth and nose caused me to jump up out of the bed but I was being pinned down.

"I should break your fucking neck for this stunt," King said as he stared in my eyes with his pretty brown eyes that were looking dark and scary. I squirmed and tried my best to get him off of me.

"I'm going to let you up but you better not swing," he said through gritted teeth. He let me go and I sat up on the side of the bed.

"I can't believe you, Gucci. How could you just leave like that?"

"Please leave, King. I don't want to fight with you. Just let me go on and live my life." I had my head down because I didn't want him to see me crying.

"What the fuck you mean by let you go? You're crazy if you think I'm letting you or my daughter leave. So, get off this bullshit, pack your shit, and let's go. I really don't understand why you're doing this." He sat on the side of me and was trying to pull me in closer."

"It's really sad that you don't understand what I'm going through. That's why it's best I walk away from this one sided ass relationship." I got up and went to the kitchen to get a bottle of water.

"Would you please stop talking in fucking code and tell me what's on your mind. I hate it when you do that and you know it."

"It's obvious that you hate a lot of things about me. That's why you can't commit."

"Here we go with this shit again. Stop trying to change me. I'm a grown ass man."

I couldn't do nothing but laugh at that last statement.

"You think this funny, huh?" He stepped in my face and I stepped back some. I knew he wanted to swing on me.

"What's funny is you coming up in here acting like shit is all good between us. Bye King. I'm not doing this with you right now."

I tried walking past him but he grabbed me and threw me into the wall. He was so close in my face that the Double mint gum on his breath sent a cool breeze up my nose.

"Stop fucking playing with me before I beat your ass up in here. As a matter of fact, I'm done playing with you. Since you took Imani from me, I'm taking her from you."

He walked past me and out of the door. He slammed it hard as hell. I just slid to the floor and cried. I didn't cry because he took Imani. King is a wonderful father to our daughter. It really hurts my heart because he doesn't understand how his actions affect me.

****

"Earth to Gucci. What are you over there thinking about?" Dior asked.

We were out shopping for the Thug Inc. anniversary party. I am in no mood to go because I don't want to see King.

"I was thinking about Imani. I miss my baby."

"If you miss her so much, go and get her. It's been two weeks now. I think you've proven your point. You need to make things right with King before one of these bitches bump your spot. I heard he's been fucking with that hoe Samaya. "Why would you tell her something like that, Dior? Your ass is messy. She doesn't have to make up with him if she doesn't want to. King needs to shit or get the off the pot," Chanel said as we walked inside the dress shop to get fitted for our custom-made gowns.

I didn't respond to either one of them. Hearing Samaya's name had me hot. She has been running behind King since high school. She's the spokesperson for thirsty bitches. I have kicked her ass so many times it isn't funny. She isn't even worth the fight anymore.

Dior wrapped her arms around my shoulder. "I'm sorry, G. I wasn't trying to be messy."

"It's cool. Let's just get our dresses and get out of here. I'm ready to go home." I just wanted to sleep away all my problems.

"You need to get out of the house. Your ass is getting thicker than a Snicker staying in the house eating up everything in sight. Tonight is Rahmeek's party at Gentlemen's Paradise. You should go with us. Please don't say you don't want to go because of King.

While you're in the house sulking, that nigga is out enjoying life. You need to show him what he's missing. Now let's put on our freak'um dresses and party," Chanel said as she thumbed through the racks of dresses.

"Okay, I'm going. I'm telling you now, if King tries to show out, it's going to be some shit. Real talk."

After shopping for a couple of more hours, I went home and took a long nap. It was ten at night when I woke up. I slept longer than I intended to. I immediately started to get ready. I bet Chanel and Dior think I'm not coming. I'm going to surprise them.

Once I was dressed, I looked at myself in the floor length mirror. Chanel was right. My ass and titties were bigger. My dress was so short that my ass cheeks were playing peek-a-boo. King was definitely going to get an eyeful. My red bottoms had my legs looking real nice. Trish had my hair on point as usual. I loved my twenty-six inch Peruvian sew-in. After checking my makeup and my clothes, I was out the door and on my way to party. The line was wrapped around the corner. It was a good thing that I was plugged. I was too bad of a female to stand in a line.

The party was jumping when I walked in. I went straight up to V.I.P to find my sisters I ran into King sitting in a booth with Samaya on his lap. As soon as our eyes connected, he pushed that bitch off of him so hard she hit the floor. I just laughed and walked away. I didn't have time for his shit. I found the rest of the wives and got ready to turn up.

"What's up, bitch? I thought you had changed your mind," Chanel said as she poured her a shot of pineapple Ciroc.

"My ass fell asleep."

"You're looking good as fuck. Did King see you with your ass all out?" Dior asked as she sipped her drink.

"Fuck King! I have no words for him. I walked in and Samaya was sitting on his lap. As soon as he saw me, he pushed that hoe off of him. I'm not fucking with him, period. Hand me the bottle, bitches. I'm about to get my drink on."

Chapter 3 - King

Let's Straighten It Out

The last thing I needed was for Gucci to see Samaya sitting on my lap. It was bad enough are relationship had been strained. I had been trying my best to talk to her. I didn't know what else to do. She definitely wasn't about to deal with a nigga after seeing that. I could kick Samaya's ass. I had to order another bottle of Ace of Spades. Gucci not fucking with me had me off my square.

"What's up, my nigga?" Malik said as he came and sat next to me.

"I'm good, bro. This situation with Gucci is fucking up my mental.

"Trust me, I've been there. Gucci is down for you. Don't be no fool. That cheating shit ain't where it's at. I'm a living witness. That shit could have disastrous consequences. The street life is hectic. You need a good woman to come home to after a hard day's work. You better wife Gucci before it's too late. Don't look now, but there's a nigga on the dance floor with her now. Malik said as his eyes went to the dance floor.

I had steam coming out my ears as I saw this ass nigga feeling all over Gucci. When she bent over, I could see her ass cheeks. That was it. I walked out of VIP and straight to the dance floor. I wanted to knock the nigga out but I didn't want to disrespect my nigga Rah. I picked her ass up and threw her over my shoulder.

"Put me down right now, King. I'm not playing with you!"

She was yelling and screaming at the top of her lungs as I carried her out of the club.

"Shut that ass up!" I said as I smacked her on her exposed ass. That made me even madder. Out here in these streets showing my goodies to these niggas.

"What the fuck is wrong with you, G?"

"I simply don't give a fuck. Just like you. Let me go so I can finish turning up."

She was trying her best to get past me. She was drunk as hell and that wasn't a good look because she didn't even drink like that.

"You're finished turning up. Get the in the car before I put your ass in there."

She stood there with her arms folded so I picked her up and put her in the car.

"I swear to God, I hate you," she said.

I didn't respond because I knew she was speaking out of anger. As we drove away from the club, I noticed her crying. She had been doing a lot of that lately. I knew that I was the reason why and I needed to change things. Malik was right. I needed to get my shit together before it's too late. I really didn't know what to say so I just cut the radio on. *Stay* by T.I and Victoria Monet was playing. The lyrics fit perfectly for us at that very moment. I reached over and grabbed Gucci's hand but she snatched it away.

"Why are we going this way? My house is in the opposite direction."

"I want you to come home with me. Me and Imani miss you, Ma."

Gucci continued to ignore me and stare out of the window. Shortly after, we pulled up to my crib and went inside the house. She went straight to the guest bedroom and slammed the door. This has got to end. It was four in the morning and I decided to make few calls. I needed to make things right with Gucci.

Chapter 4 - Gucci

A New Us

The next morning I woke up to the sound of someone banging on the door. I instantly sat up, but I had to quickly lie back down because my head hurt. I drank too much last night. I'm a wine kind of girl. I don't even do hard liquor. I just needed something to clear my head. Now I'm paying for it. For a minute, I forgot where I was. Then it dawned on me that King kidnapped me. I laughed to myself as I remembered him carrying me over his shoulder.

The beating on the door did not stop until I got up to answer it. King came out of his room with a towel wrapped around his waist at the same time. He looked so good to me. The feeling in Ms. Kitty let me know she needed some attention.

"That better not be one of your bitches or it's about to be go up in this motherfucker!"

"Calm your ass down," King walked pass me and went downstairs to open the front door. He flung the door open. It was Nasir with a patch on his head.

"What the hell happened to you?" I asked as I rushed over to him. He had blood all over his shirt.

"Me and Chanel got into it on our way home from the club, we got to tussling in the car. I lost control and ran into a fucking tree. Thank God, we both had on our seat belts. I'm done with that bitch."

Here we go again with this bullshit. Every other week they're fighting and in the E.R. My relationship with King ain't nothing compared to Nasir and Chanel's. King had already walked away. He was fed up with my sister and his brother. Their drama is never ending and we always seem to be in the middle of it.

"Where is she right now?"

"Her ass is at home. The airbag messed her face up. That's what she gets for starting shit all the time. I can't take the bitch no-where without her acting stupid. If a chick looks at me too long, she wants to fight her and me. Chanel has to stop being so inse-cure. I love her but I'm ready to call it quits.

Nasir got up and went upstairs. I really need to talk to Chanel because I have never heard him say the things, he just said about her. That would have to be later on because my head was hurting bad as hell. I went inside King's bathroom to find some aspirin. I looked inside the medicine cabinet but they weren't there. I was about to go ask him where they were when I noticed the bottle sitting on his nightstand. I went to grab it and noticed a box of Magnums lying on the floor beside the bed.

I picked up the box. Two were missing. All I could do was shake my head. I wasn't even mad. I knew that we hadn't had sex in a minute. King couldn't go without sex. So, I knew he was getting it from somewhere. I just took the pill and lay across his bed. The smell of his Issey Miyake cologne invaded my nostrils and helped me to drift off to sleep.

*****

"Wake up, G."

The sound of King's deep voice and the feel of his soft lips pressed against mine brought me out of my slumber. "Come on and get dressed I have a surprise for you." He walked out of the room and returned with shopping bags.

I sat up in bed and looked at him. "What's all of this and where are we going?" He didn't answer. He just walked out of the room then came back with Imani.

I took her out of King's arms and held her so tight. "Hey baby. Momma missed you so much."

"Hi Mommy. Get dressed. Daddy has a surprise for you."

I looked over at King. He had wicked grin on his face. I wasn't sure what he was up to but I was not in the mood for his games. I wanted to grab Imani and run up out of there. I'm tired of King and his shit. On the other hand, I just want to be here with him and our daughter. I miss the way we used to be.

"Come on, Imani. Give Mommy some privacy. We'll be downstairs waiting on you, G."

I love when he calls me G. the way he says it makes me fall in love with him all over again. I looked inside the bags. There was a True Religion outfit along with a pair of white and pink Air Force Ones. I took a long shower and was ready to head out the door. I wondered what the hell King was up to. We had been driving for some time. Imani had fallen asleep and I was tired of sitting on my ass.

"Where are we going King?"

As soon as the words left my mouth, we pulled up into the driveway of a huge house. There were other beautiful homes all around. The big black gate was beautiful with the big gold letters K and G on the front. I watched as King put a code into the security pad. The gates opened up and we drove up to the front of the house. I stared out of the window in amazement. King grabbed my hand and kissed the back of it.

"I know that you haven't really been feeling me lately. That had me fucked up because you're my heart and soul. Knowing that you just up and left like that hurt a nigga. I've realized that I never want to live without ya'll. I want to wake up and go to sleep each and every day with my two favorite girls. Do you still want us to live together?"

I was silent for a minute because I was trying to take in what King had said.

"Of course I want us to live together. At the same time, it makes no sense to move in together if you're going to still fuck other bitches. I want all of you. If you can't commit to that then let's just co-parent and keep it like that."

"You got that, Gucci. It's just Imani and us. No more bullshit. Are we good?"

I wanted so badly to believe King but I knew there was a bitch stashed somewhere. For now, I would just be happy that we're working towards making our relationship work. "Yeah. We're good."

I blushed then grabbed his face and kissed his lips. I made sure to suck on his bottom lip like he loved for me to do.

"In that case, Welcome Home. Let's go inside so I can give ya'll a tour."

"Oh my God! Is this really our house?" I said as we walked into the house.

The house was black, gold, and fully furnished. It was luxurious. I didn't want to put Imani down because I feared she might break something. There were glass and crystal figurines everywhere; African American art was all over the walls. There was a big portrait of us hanging over the fireplace. I was confused because that picture hung over my bed at my new apartment.

"I already know what you're thinking. I moved all of your things in here. I had your Mom and Dior come and help me decorate. Some of my workers helped me move everything. We managed to get it all done during the night and earlier today."

"You just knew I was going to say yeah huh?"

He grabbed me and hugged me so tight. "I wasn't sure, but I was going to kidnap your ass if you said no."

We both laughed and continued the tour. I absolutely loved our room. It was huge. His side of the room was Scarface themed and mine was Marilyn Monroe themed. He knows that I love her. It was great that he had his own bathroom and closet and I had mine. I hate sharing bathrooms with King. He takes forever to get dressed. We went to see Imani's room.

"Look Mommy! It's Princess Elsa." King had got her a life size Elsa. The entire room looked like the movie *Frozen*.

"Everything is so nice, Bae. I can't believe you did all of this for us."

"There's nothing my two favorite girls can't have. You already know that, G. Everything you need is here. I need to handle some business. I'll be back later. Hit me up if you need me. I love you so much. You know that right?"

I shook my head as he pulled me close by my belt loops. "I love you too."

He kissed me then walked out of the house. I sat on the bed and took in everything. This was what I wanted. However, I had this feeling that something was lurking in the shadows and had the potential to ruin things. I quickly shook the thoughts from my head. I had to get all those negative thoughts from my mind and let the positive things takeover.

Since Imani was in her room playing and King was gone, I decided to look at the rest of the house. Our backyard was huge. It had a rose garden and a gazebo. We had a huge swimming pool, a movie theater, and an indoor Jacuzzi. It was so beautiful. All I could do was smile. King had gone all out with this house.

The previous night of partying and drinking had taken a toll on me. I got Imani ready for bed then I took a shower and climbed into bed. Nothing was on cable so I decided to watch Netflix. I love watching Orange is the New Black. It's crazy and funny as hell. I got sleepy so I cut the TV off and drifted off to sleep.

The feeling of my body being jerked towards the end of the bed caused me to jump out of my sleep. A man was standing at the foot of my bed dressed in all black with a ski-mask on.

"Who the fuck are you?" I yelled.

"I'm the Pussy Bandit and I came to take the pussy."

"My man will be home any minute so you better hurry up and leave. He don't play about other niggas trying to get his pussy."

"Fuck that nigga!" he said. In one swift motion, he pushed both of my legs behind my head and rammed his entire dick inside of me.

"Ahhhhh!" I screamed out at the pain. He slowly began to fuck the shit out of me.

"That nigga don't lay pipe like this. Tell me how much you love this dick."

"I love this dick!" I screamed as he roughly grabbed my face and made me look into his eyes. He shoved his tongue in my mouth and continued to ram his dick inside of me. I felt myself cum all over his dick. I felt like a leaking faucet.

"That's right, cum all over this dick. Come here. Show me how much you love this dick."

He stood up and I crawled to the foot of the bed. I took his dick in my mouth and began to make mad passionate love to it with my tongue. The slurping, gagging, and sucking sounds were driving this nigga crazy. I could hear the sound of him grunting as he released all his seeds down my throat. I rose up and pulled the ski mask from his face.

"What's up, Pussy Bandit? I missed this dick," I said as I kissed his lips.

"I missed that pussy. I can tell she missed me as well," King said as got undressed and laid in bed next to me.

I loved it when we role-played. Our sex life was the shit when we weren't beefing. As soon as we both got comfortable, his phone started to ring. He ignored it for as long as he could until finally, he answered. I listened as King spoke in codes. I laid there wondering if it was another female.

"I need to head back out and handle this little situation. I'll be back before you know it."

He tried to kiss me on the lips, but I turned my head and his lips landed on my jaw. He knew I was pissed about him leaving.

"Don't start that shit, G. You know that when the streets call, I have to go. I know you're thinking there's another bitch, but it's not. I meant what I said earlier. It's all about you and Imani."

He tried to kiss my lips again. This time I let him. I slipped my tongue in his mouth so that I could savor the taste of him. Once King was gone, I stared at the ceiling. I knew that late hours came with being with a nigga like King. It was different when we didn't live together. I felt a certain type of way about him leaving back out at five in the morning. I wanted him in my life and that meant that I wanted everything that came along with being with him. I made it up in my mind that I would make it my business not to nag him or be insecure. While King was out conquering the streets, I would fall back and be the ride or die bitch he needed by his side.

Chapter 5 - King

Niggas Are Gossiping

I had been waiting for the call that I had just received. Dutch and Nasir finally caught up with that bitch ass nigga Rocko. I hated to leave Gucci like that but business comes first. She will have to get used to me keeping late hours. As I rode to meet up with Dutch and Nasir. I thought about all the things I had been hearing in the streets about Rocko.

He's been talking shit and gossiping about Thug Inc. like a bitch. What real nigga does shit like that? He's been in his feelings ever since I gave his ass a leg shot for selling on a corner that he knew belonged to me. That was disrespectful. I hate blatant disrespect. Niggas already know the streets are run by Thug Inc. Anything getting sold better have our stamp of approval on it.

The nigga knew from the jump that he was violating. That leg shot wasn't enough though. Now he has to pay with his life. We no longer had the warehouse that Thug had used. Over the years, we had killed so many people there that it started to smell like death. We now owned and operated our own Public Storage facility. We didn't rent any spaces out to the public though. Each space served a purpose for our organization. When Thug became Mob Boss, he cut a lot of niggas loose and he always wanted to stay a step ahead of the law.

I parked in my parking space and entered the main entrance that led down to the torture chamber. It was built underground and the entire facility was soundproof.

"What's up my niggas?" I said as I walked into room.

Nasir and Dutch were sitting on a table smoking a blunt. Rocko was hanging from the ceiling by chains. He was naked and bloody. I didn't know if he was dead or unconscious. I hoped they hadn't killed his ass yet.

"You'll never guess where we caught this nigga," Nasir said as he handed the blunt to me.

"Enlighten me."

"This motherfucker was getting out of the car with Detective Jones."

"That's not good. There is no telling what the fuck he been running his mouth about. It's a must we He's becoming a big problem," I said as I inhaled deeply. I needed Thug to give me the go ahead to murk his ass.

"I knew there was a reason I didn't like this nigga. Fuck this shit. I need to get home to Dior. You niggas pussy footing around," Dutch said as he jumped off the table and grabbed an electric handsaw. He walked over to Rocko and started slicing into his skin. The pain caused him to jump and wail.

"I thought your ass was dead, nigga," I laughed.

I wanted to talk to him but he was no condition to say anything since Dutch's crazy ass was slicing into him like he was carving a turkey.

"Lower that motherfucker down to the floor!"

Nasir and Dutch started pulling the chains. I walked over to the table and grabbed a box cutter before putting on leather gloves.

"This is what happens to niggas who have loose lips. See you in hell, you snitch ass nigga."

I pried his mouth open and cut his tongue out of his mouth. I placed it inside a box and made sure to address it to his mother. She should have taught him to

"Call the cleanup crew. Let's hit up White Palace for some breakfast. I'm hungry as fuck," Dutch said as fired up another blunt.

We all left and went to the restaurant. It was almost eight in the morning. I was anxious to get back home and get back up inside Gucci. Hopefully, she wasn't pissed off at me.

Chapter 6 - Gucci

It's A Celebration

It had been a month since King and I moved in together. Things have been so good between us. No arguing or fighting. I have been on cloud nine and nothing could bring me down. Since moving in together, all we do is stay cooped up in our bedroom fucking each other's brains out. I was glad my mother had Imani majority of the time. King and I needed some us time and we got it without interruption. Nasir and Dutch ran things while he catered to me. Of course I knew that shit would end. I understood though. Niggas out in the streets would think it was sweet if he stayed away too long.

It was finally the night of the Thug Inc. anniversary party and it was all over the social networks. Too bad that it was invitation only. I kept looking at myself in the mirror. I wanted to be perfect. My hair was in long cascading spiral curls. I was rocking a black Versace dress that dipped low in the back and front. I had all gold crystal encrusted Giuseppe Zanotti's on my feet with the matching clutch.

"You look so good, Ma. I want to snatch that dress off you and say fuck that party. Let's have our own party." King pulled me in close and started tugging at my dress.

"No, King. You're going to wrinkle my dress and mess up my makeup."

I wiggled free from his grip and straightened up his bowtie. He was looking as handsome as ever in his black Gucci tux and matching loafers. My baby looked like money for real.

"You're so handsome," I said looking into his beautiful eyes. We kissed each other passionately. We were lost in the moment until we were rudely interrupted.

"Hop off the dick, Gucci. Let's go before we have to stand in line," Chanel said as she drank champagne from her flute.

"We don't stand in lines. Make that your last glass of champagne before we leave. The night is still young and I don't want you drunk early. The last thing I need is you embarrassing yourself and me," Nasir said as he walked out of the living room.

Chanel just stood there speechless and that was a first. Something was definitely going on with them. I really need to talk to Chanel and see what the fuck is going on with them. I've been so wrapped up in my own relationship that I have been neglecting Dior and Chanel.

The stretch Hummer limo was already outside. Dior and Dutch were inside already all over each other.

"Ughh! Get a room," I said as I kissed her and hugged Dutch.

"Hey ya'll, what's up?" Dutch said as he dapped up Nasir and King.

We sipped champagne and smoked some blunts as we rode to the party. I was feeling real good and looking beautiful. King and I were officially a couple and I wanted the world to know. It had been so long since I've been out partying with him. This would be a test of our relationship. There was a time when we could never party without me beating a bitch up or him dragging me out the club and whooping my ass for dancing with a nigga. I didn't want that to be us anymore.

****

The sound of Young Thug's song *Lifestyle* boomed throughout the banquet hall as we walked the red carpet. Tahari had gone all out and the hall was beautiful. The decorations were all white and black with Swarovski crystals draping over everything. Everyone looked so good in their clothes. Once we went to the VIP section reserved for us, Nasir, Dutch, and King went to mingle with their business associates. They made sure they had bottles sent to the table to keep us occupied. Chanel couldn't wait to drink some more. I prayed she didn't start any shit.

"Slow down, Chanel. You're drinking too fast. Please don't start any mess tonight. This about our niggas. They worked hard for this night." I told her, snatching the bottle of Ace of Spades out of her hand.

"Please don't act a fool up in here," Dior said.

"Both of ya'll can shut the fuck up. I'm sick and tired of everybody ganging up on me about my behavior. It's cool though. I'm good on ya'll for the rest of the night. I'll make sure to stay as far away from ya'll as possible."

Chanel snatched the bottle from my hand and walked over to sit with Barbie. They were really close, mainly because they were both loud and had no problem showing their asses. Barbie was cool though. We fuck with her the long way.

The sound of clapping and whistling made me quickly forget about Chanel and her bratty behavior. Thug and Tahari had finally arrived and everyone was standing to their feet showing them their respect. I must say they looked so good together. They complimented one another. They were truly Bonnie and Clyde. I wanted that type of love with King but I knew it wasn't going to be easy. Over the years Tahari and Thug had been through hell and back. I wondered what was in store for King and me.

"Come on, G. You know that's my song right there," Dior said as she stood up and grabbed my hand and led me to the dance floor.

Fancy by Iggy Azalea was playing. The dance floor was packed with the majority of bitches. As Dior and I danced to the music, I kept feeling someone bumping into me. I looked over to my right and it was the bitch Samaya. I instantly became pissed and Dior sensed it.

"Fuck that bitch, G. Catch that bitch next time. You already know King ain't checking for her ass. That's why she mad."

Dior grabbed my hand and we continued to dance through three more songs. The entire time Samaya and her mutt ass friends were trying their best to get some shit started, but I wasn't about to ruin my baby's night.

"The next time I see that bitch I'm whooping her ass. I was heated as we sat back down at our table.

"Yes, that bitch is cruising for a bruising. She gon' get exactly what she looking for. Come on, let's find King so we can put him up on game."

Dior was the calm one out of all of us. She would knock a bitch out though if she needed to. All that fighting with Dutch taught her how to give a bitch a one-hitter quitter. I couldn't believe that they were all in the back of the hall shooting dice in their Tux's. Tahari came back there and went off.

"I know motherfucking well ya'll ain't shooting dice. Thug bring your ass here. We need to talk."

"Go head on with that bullshit, Ta-Baby. This is a fucking celebration in honor of me and my niggas Take your ass on somewhere." Thug never even looked up from the dice game.

"Whatever, Ka'Jaire. Fuck you and this party," Tahari said as she stormed off with Thug on her heels.

"Boss Lady about to get all in that nigga shit," Dutch laughed as he stopped shooting dice and wrapped his arms around Dior's waist.

"What's up, G? Are you enjoying yourself?"

I thought about telling him about the bitch Samaya but I decided against it.

"I'm good. I just wanted to come and check on you."

I kissed him as he grabbed a handful of my ass. "I have to use the washroom. I'll be right back." I went to the bathroom and went straight into the stall.

"Ohhh baby. This shit feels so good."

"You love when I fuck you like this, don't you?"

I couldn't believe my ears Thug and Tahari were fucking in the damn stall. I had to cover my mouth to keep from laughing. I quickly handled my business and got the hell out of there. As soon as I walked out the bathroom, I walked right into pandemonium. Dior and Barbie were holding Chanel back and Dutch was holding Nasir back. Chanel was crying.

"How could you do this to me Nasir?"

"I'm not trying to hear that shit. Get her out of here now! Drunk bitch." Nasir's words dripped with venom. I loved him like a brother but he didn't have to disrespect my sister like that.

"Really Nasir? You don't have to disrespect her like that. That shit ain't cool. What the hell is going on anyway?" I asked as I tried to help Dior and Barbie drag Chanel out of the party.

"Her stupid ass just walked up to me and slapped the shit out of me. I'm done with her stupid ass."

Nasir yanked away from Dutch and went straight to the bar. I looked at King and pleaded for him to go talk to Nasir. Reluctantly, he went after him. I knew King was pissed at their behavior.

"Let me the fuck go!"

Chanel yanked away from all of us and ran out of the hall. We were trying our best to catch up with her but she hopped in a cab and left. I really wanted to hop in a cab and follow her but I wasn't ready to leave. Plus, I wasn't about to leave King here with all these thirsty bitches. We stayed and partied for the rest of the night. I couldn't wait until the next day I was going to dig all in Chanel's shit. She needed to let me know what was going on with her.

Chapter 7 - Chanel Lennox

Crazy In Love

I cried the entire ride home. I couldn't believe I caught Samina giving Nasir head in the men's bathroom. That bitch was slick just like her hoe ass sister Samaya. I watched as he got up and went to the bathroom. Not long after she got up and went into the bathroom. I immediately got up and went inside the bathroom as well. They were so caught up in the moment that they never heard me come in. All I could hear was him moaning her name and telling her how good her mouth felt.

I was so sick to my stomach that I threw up in the garbage can outside of the bathroom. I walked around looking for my **sisters** to tell them what had happened. I had to get out of there because I was about to kill him and that bitch. I couldn't find Dior or Gucci anywhere. I saw them coming out of the bathroom like it was nothing and I lost my cool.

I slapped the fuck out him and commenced to kicking her ass. I felt someone yank be my hair and spin me around. The slap Nasir gave me caused me to hit the floor instantly. I never got a chance to hit his ass back because they pulled us a part. Mina was smiling at how Nasir was disrespecting me. He treated me like a random bitch in the street and that shit hurt my soul.

Nasir has no idea that I know about him cheating on me with her. About a year ago, I went through his phone and found naked pictures of her. I read their messages and found out that they were meeting up at the hotel. I followed him and sure enough, they went inside the Best Western. A cheap ass hotel for a cheap ass hoe. Every week they meet up on Thursday. Since I found out about them, I have immersed myself in a liquor bottle. As long as I'm drunk, I'm numb to the pain.

I'm still trying to figure why I put up with his bullshit. I confided in my mother and told her about Nasir cheating. She told me that I needed to do a better job at keeping Nasir satisfied. I really despised her submissive attitude. That prostitute mentality was getting really old. I was crushed behind her advice. I knew that I was being the best woman I could be to him. He was just being a typical no good nigga. His behavior tonight let me know it was a wrap for us. I was too drunk to move out of the home we shared tonight. All the crying mixed with the alcohol had my head banging. All I wanted to do was sleep. I peeled out of my dress and lay across the bed with nothing but my panties and bra on.

****

"Wake up, Chanel!"

My eyes fluttered as I slowly opened them up and realized Nasir was standing over me. I cringed at the sight of him. I rolled over and turned my back on him. I was hurting so bad I didn't want him to see me crying.

"I can't do this anymore, Chanel. I think it's best we separate for a little while."

Nasir was sitting on the side of the bed. He still had on his tuxedo. It was disheveled, but he was still sexy as ever. His dreads were hanging down almost covering his cute light-skinned baby face. I immediately crawled out of the bed and went to handle my personal hygiene without speaking a word to his ass. There really was no need for any words. He had said more than enough.

I splashed water on my face to calm myself down. I felt like I was about to have a heart attack and pass out. Flashbacks of happier times invaded my mind. Then fear of the unknown set in. How do I move on from my first everything? I slid down the wall and sat on the floor. I was trying to comprehend Nasir's words. I couldn't believe I was so broken. The feisty Chanel had been replaced with a weak ass bitch that let a nigga and his side bitch play her. I was becoming angry and I wanted to tear some shit up. Reality set in and I knew acting a fool wouldn't help me.

I slowly got up and finished handling my personal hygiene. I slowly walked out of the bathroom and into my walk in closet. I grabbed my Louis Vuitton luggage and packed as much as I could. I had no intention of ever returning. It took me a couple of trips up and down the stairs. Nasir, Dutch, and King were sitting on the couch smoking like it was nothing. I began carrying my things out and placing them in my trunk and the backseat.

Before I peeled out of the driveway, I looked back at my house. I tried not to cry but the tears were falling rapidly. I had my head down in my hands. I was crying so hard and loud. It was one of those ugly cries with snot running all over the place. The sound of someone banging on my window caused me to look up.

"Open the door. Let me holla at you for a minute," Nasir said pulling on the door handle.

At that moment, I had nothing but hatred in my heart for his ass. I started my car and drove away. I don't know how I ended up on the expressway and headed out of Chicago. This was the last place I wanted to be. I don't know how I ended up in Columbus, Georgia. I checked myself into Stay Bridge Suites. I paid to stay for a month. My goal was to get on my feet and call my family later. I hated to just up and leave on my sisters but how could I stand being around them while they were with King and Dutch? Hopefully, they would understand. I had to do what was best for me.

Chapter 8 - Dior Lennox

Forceful Decisions

I was nervous as I sat on the couch in my living room. I kept looking at the pregnancy test hoping that one of the pink lines would disappear. I knew that it wouldn't though. I had been sick for the last two weeks. It was easy for me to hide the morning sickness because Dutch is always gone. I couldn't tell him that I needed to make a doctor's appointment. He would want to know why and he would want to go with me. I didn't need him acting a fool because the doctor needed to look inside me. He had already beaten my last doctor's ass because he felt like the man was enjoying it.

Most women would be happy that they're pregnant with their first child. That's not the case for me. I'm actually petrified knowing that I am. When I first got with Dominique "Dutch" Johnson, he made it perfectly clear that he never wanted kids. We were teenagers and having fun, but now we're older and married. I agreed because I was seventeen years old and didn't want kids either. The warmth I felt right now inside my heart let me know that I want this baby.

Dutch is going to go ballistic. That's the last thing I want. Dutch has a really bad temper. He has learned to control his temper over the years. I steer clear of his ass when he gets like that. He's a different type of animal when he's mad. Dutch had a fucked up childhood. He has never gone into details, but I can tell that there is some serious shit going on inside of him. Regardless of his flaws, I love him with all my heart and I know that he feels the same way about me. Dutch resembles the rapper Nelly. He's cockier though. He has a perfect set of white teeth. I love how he keeps his hair cut low. His waves are so deep they make a bitch seasick just from looking at them.

From the first time we met I knew he was the one for me. It's a crazy but funny story. Gucci and I had got our first jobs at McDonalds. We had only been working there a week. On this particular day it was so busy. I was working on the register. It was kind of hard because I was still learning how to use it. Plus, I had to get my customers orders ready. I was fucking up some shit big time. Gucci was working doing the same thing, only her ass had the shit down pact. Our supervisor was being a real bitch. Hollering at me in front of the customers and shit. I wanted to curse his ass out bad. I knew I couldn't though. My momma insisted we get a job and keep it. She was tired of selling her ass. Dutch stepped in my line and King was in Gucci's.

"You're too fucking pretty to be working up in this motherfucker?" Dutch said as he licked his lips.

"Well pretty doesn't pay the bills. So, this is what I have to do." He was getting ready to respond, but my bitch ass supervisor came out of nowhere and starting talking shit to me.

"You need to socialize with this Thug on your own time. Not while you're on my clock. I'm tempted to send you home anyway. Moving all slow and shit.

"Apologize to my girl for disrespecting her." Dutch said. I watched his eyes as they turned real dark and I knew it was about to be some shit. The whole restaurant was quiet waiting to see what was going to happen next. Before I knew it Dutch and King hopped over the counter and started beating the fuck out of him. I was in shock as I watched Dutch and King both poor hot ass oil on him from the fry station until he apologized to me. He finally did and after that Dutch grabbed my hand and King did the same with Gucci. We ran out the door right with their nutty asses. It's been us ever since. Now if that ain't some crazy shit. I don't know what is. When we told our mother what happened she fell in love with them. After dating them for a couple of months my mother let them come and live with us. That's how Nasir and Chanel ended together. They were young as hell getting money and all our mother saw was dollar signs. They kept her laced and the bills paid. Candy didn't have a care in the world.

*****

I heard the garage door open. I wanted to keep it from him and wait until it was too late to get an abortion but I knew that I couldn't. Dutch keeps up with my periods and he knows my pussy inside and out. If he even thinks there's a slight change, he will spazz the fuck out. I let out a deep breath and got ready to tell him I was pregnant and that I want to keep it.

"Good Morning." I said as Dutch walked inside the house and began to undress by the laundry room.

He always did that. Dutch was such a neat freak. He sat next to me on the couch. I leaned over and kissed him on the lips.

"What are you doing up this early?"

"You know I can't sleep when you're gone. I was waiting for you to come home so I can crawl in bed with you and sleep the day away like we always do."

"Let's go lay down then. A nigga tired as shit." Dutch stood up and I grabbed his hand. I placed the pregnancy test inside his hand as well.

"What the fuck is this shit, Dior!"

"I'm pregnant." I kept my head down because I was scared to look up at him.

"What the fuck you mean? Aren't you on birth control pills?"

"Yeah, I forget to take them sometimes."

"You already know how I feel about this. You need to make an appointment for an abortion."

I followed him into the bedroom. We got in the bed. I sat up with my back against the headboard. I always give Dutch his way but not this time.

"I'm keeping the baby, Dutch."

"What the fuck did you just say?' Dutch got out of bed and stood over me. I already knew what was coming next so I prepared myself for battle.

"I'm going to tell you this one time and one time only, dead that shit."

"I'm not getting an abortion. I want to keep this baby. I always do what you want. This time we're doing something that I want."

I got up from the bed and tried to walk away. Dutch grabbed my hair and pulled me back towards him.

"Who the fuck you think you talking to. You want me to beat your ass? It's been a minute since I laid hands on you. I suggest you do what the fuck I say," he said through gritted teeth. He was going to have to whoop my ass because I wasn't backing down from my decision.

"Do what you have to do, Dominique."

He hated his real name so I know that made him even madder. I pried his hands from my hair and walked away from him. Before I could walk away. I was met with a kick to my back that me to fall. I twisted my ankle as I fell. He turned me over on my back and sat on my stomach. He started raining blows all over my face and head. He was in such a rage. I couldn't believe that having a baby would make him do this to me.

"I'll get the abortion! I promise that I'll get it! Please stop, Dutch."

After hitting me a couple of more times, he finally stopped.

"Damn! I'm sorry baby. Just please get the abortion. I'm not capable of being a father to anyone."

Dutch walked out of the room and I heard him leave out of the house. I laid on the floor for a couple of minutes silently crying. Dutch had taken his anger to another level and I didn't know how things would be after this.

Chapter 9 – Dominique "Dutch" Johnson

Haunted By The Past

I drove around aimlessly trying to wrap my mind around the fact that I had just hurt Dior like that. I have always had anger issues. Being with Dior helped to calm the beast inside of me. I only like that side of me to come out when I'm handling shit in the streets. Everything inside of me was saying to go back and check on my baby but I couldn't look at her right now. I needed to clear my head. I couldn't believe that Dior was pregnant. She broke our agreement. We never wanted kids. How could she change up on me like that? Everything was good between us. Why would she fuck everything up? If she keeps the baby, I'm leaving her. A nigga like me will never be father material.

I needed to talk to someone. The only one I knew who could give me some advice was Thug. I hit him up and he told me it was cool for me to come over. After I pulled up to their gate, the armed security guards let me through. Thug wasn't playing about his family's safety. This nigga had security detail like the Obamas.

"What's good, my nigga?" he said as we dapped each other up.

"Shit is all bad on the home front." I ran my hand over face in frustration.

"Sup Uncle Dutch?" Ka'Jaire Jr. said as he dapped me up.

"What's up, lil homie?"

"Daddy, when are we going to play Call of Duty?" The boss of the house Ka'Jaiyah walked in before he could answer Jr.

"No, Daddy is having a tea party with me. Ain't that right, Daddy?" she said as she looked at him with puppy dog eyes. All of his kids came in and started pulling him in all directions.

"That's enough, ya'll. Come on, let's go in the family room. Daddy and Uncle Dutch need to talk. Daddy will play with all of ya'll later."

Tahari came and took all the kids out back with her. I was in awe of how much those kids loved him. Watching them made me really want to rethink my situation.

"How do you run the city and still manage to be a great father. Those kids love you."

"My kids and my wife mean the world to me. They balance a nigga out. The sound of my kids feet running to greet me at the door is the best feeling in the world. Being a father is a beautiful thing.

"What's going on with you, Dutch? Holla at me."

We went to his office. I had to prepare myself for what I was about to tell him. I had never discussed this with anyone, not even my mother. I knew Thug could give me the advice I needed. Their family had been through it all and he held it together. Plus, he's always been there for me like a big brother. I knew I could trust him with my secrets because I trust him with my life.

"Dior is pregnant."

"Congratulations, my nigga. Let's pop a bottle in celebration."

Thug went to grab a bottle of Remy from the fridge in his office. He placed a shot glass in front of us and filled them both to the rim.

" I don't want any kids. I told her to get an abortion."

"Please tell me you didn't do any goofy shit like that."

"I'm not father material. I have some deep shit going on with me. I've never even talked about this with Dior or my mother. I was molested by my father every chance he got. His name was Snake and he used to beat me and my mother if we breathed wrong."

"Did you say Snake?" Thug asked as he knocked back his shot.

"Unfortunately, yeah. He and Peaches were an item back in the day. "Thug knocked back another shot. I wasn't surprised that Thug and his family knew Snake. He had women all over the city.

There was no telling how many children he had fathered prior to his disappearance. I could tell Thug was still wrapping his mind around the fact that we both knew Snake. I wondered if Snake had molested him. I wouldn't dare ask though. I just continued with my story.

"The shit he did to me made me an angry ass person. Dior is the only thing that calms me. I can't believe I put my hands on her because she refused to get an abortion. I'm all fucked up behind all this shit. How can I be a father to a kid when I never had a father myself?" I knocked back a shot and poured another.

"Fuck all that shit, Dutch. Don't let that nigga control your life. You're still living and that nigga dead as a doornail. Having a kid is a beautiful thing. How do you think Dior is feeling right now? She's at home thinking that you just don't want to be a father. That shit makes you look like less of a man. We both know that ain't true. I've been watching you since you were a shorty. You're a thug to your heart. You don't play any games in these streets. Take that heart home and build a family. You're going to need your wife and kids to come home to when all this street shit is over with. Dior is a good girl. Go home and make that shit right." Thug poured us another shot and we knocked them back.

"You said Snake was dead. I thought his ass just abandoned us."

"Ain't no coming back from what happened to him."

The look in his eyes let me know he offed his ass. I knew that there was more to the story about Snake but I really didn't care what happened to his ass. We finished the bottle and I got ready to get home. I had to make shit right with Dior. Having a baby just might be the thing I need to tame the beast that lives inside of me.

When I pulled up to our house, I was happy to see her truck in the driveway. I noticed that the house was pitch black. I went upstairs and Dior was sitting up in bed with her foot elevated and a towel covering her face.

I wanted to walk right out the door but then I would really be acting like a coward. I heard light snoring coming from her so I knew that she was asleep. I didn't want to disturb her so I went to the guest bedroom. I would just talk to her in the morning about everything.

Chapter 10 - Dior
The Point of It All

I heard Dutch when he came in the house last night. I played sleep on his ass. I had no words for him then and I definitely don't have any for him now. I had been lying in bed all morning because I was in so much pain. I had numerous knots on my head from him punching me repeatedly. Not to mention my swollen lips. I was happy that I didn't have a broken nose or black eyes. I had the headache from hell and all I wanted to do was sleep. However, my body wouldn't let me. I had the urge to pee and I didn't want to get out of bed because of my swollen ankle. I couldn't hold it any longer so I got up and attempted to go to the bathroom. As soon as I stood to my feet, liquid started running down my legs. At first, I thought it was pee until I looked down. Blood was pouring out of me. I tried to sit back on the bed but I noticed a big blood stain.

"Oh my God!" I screamed as a wave of excruciating pain hit me in my stomach causing my knees to buckle. I tried my best to stay standing but I became weak and nauseous. I started to vomit clear liquid.

"Dior! What's wrong, baby?" Dutch said as he came into the room. "Oh shit, Ma. You need to go to the hospital."

He lifted me off of the floor, put me inside the tub, and washed me up from head to toe. No words were spoken between us. There was really nothing to say. We both knew what had happened. I was having a miscarriage and he was the cause of it.

He dressed me and carried me downstairs to the car. I could still feel the blood pouring out. I wanted to cry but I refused to let the tears fall. How could Dutch do this to us? It bothered me that he still hadn't said a word about putting his hands on me or for killing our child.

"Do you want me to call your Momma and Gucci?" he asked without looking at me.

"No, I don't want anybody to know."

My mother would find a way to take up for Dutch and my sister would probably jump on his ass. Plus, this is embarrassing. I just want to go to the hospital, get checked out, and go home. The doctor confirmed that I indeed had a miscarriage. I was happy the baby had passed already because I didn't want to have a D&C. He gave me some pain meds and sent me home.

The next week or two was a blur. I had cut everybody completely off. I locked myself in my bedroom and I only came out when Dutch was gone. I couldn't stand to look at him or be around him. He was trying his best to talk to me and make me feel better. In my heart, I knew that he regretted what happened. I just wasn't ready to forgive him. Losing my baby and not knowing where the hell Chanel was had me fucked up in the head. Depression sunk in and started to get the best of me.

*****

"Baby, we really need to talk." Dutch came into the guest bedroom where I had been sleeping.

"We don't have anything to talk about."

"You don't have to say shit if you don't want to. Just let me say what I have to say. After that, if you're done with me, I'll stop trying to fix this shit.'

"Dutch, you can't bring our baby back."

"I know that, baby. I'm so fucked up behind this shit. You just don't know."

Dutch was kneeling on the side of the bed.

I had never seen him like this so I was surprised that he was showing emotion in front of me. I could have sworn I saw tears in his eyes. I rubbed the back of his head. Dutch wrapped his hands around my waist and held me. I could tell he was really fucked up. He stood up and sat beside me on the bed. I had a blunt inside the nightstand so I grabbed it and flamed it up. I took a long pull off then handed it to him. He puffed it and sat in silence.

"I was molested when I was kid by my father. I haven't seen or heard from him since I was about eight years old. I've been fucked up in the head ever since. I don't know how to be a father because he was never a father to me. I'm so scared to raise a child out of the fear that I won't be a good father. I vowed to never bring a child into my life. I'm not good at that shit."

Dutch had tears streaming from his eyes and so did I. I couldn't believe he was holding all this in. I've heard him talk about Snake and how he used to beat his mother's ass. He never mentioned being molested.

"Dutch you're going to be a great father one day. What he did to you was wrong. It's not your fault. I'm so sorry this happened to you. I just wish you had told me this sooner. It helps me to better understand why you didn't want a baby. However, it doesn't change the fact you killed our baby." I was holding his face in my hands as I spoke to him.

"I know it doesn't change anything. I swear that I'm going to do everything in my power to fix this shit. I can't bring the baby back. Just give me a chance to make shit right."

I nodded my head. I knew that things would be different between us. I had no idea how true those words would be. Without warning, I punched his ass right in the eye and followed up with a slap to his face.

"What the fuck you hit me for?"

"That's for putting your hands on me. The next time you even think about swinging on me, your ass better think twice. I am not your punching bag. Don't you ever do no shit like that to me again. Now get your ass out of my room."

"I deserved that but why can't you come and sleep in the bed with me."

"Because that room has a bad memory in it. I suggest you buy me a new house if you have plans on sleeping next to me. I want a big backyard and a swimming pool too."

"You got it. I'll start looking first thing in the morning. I love you, Dior."

"I love you too."

Dutch kissed me on the forehead and walked out of the room.

I would have been knocked the hell out of him, if I had known I would get a new house that easily.

Chapter 11 - Nasir Carter

Consequences and Repercussions

It's been months since Chanel disappeared. I know that I hurt her by asking her to leave. I was just tired of the fighting and arguing. I've been in love with Chanel since I was fifteen years old. The first time I laid eyes on her, I knew she would be my wife one day. Now that day may never come because I fucked up big time. I waited until she had all of her bags packed before I went upstairs. I found a message that on our bedroom mirror the day she left.

I hope you and that bitch Samina live a happy fucking life. I know all about you cheating on me with that bitch. I hope it was worth it you bum ass nigga.

She even left her lip prints on the mirror. I know it's my fault that she's MIA. I just want her to let her mother and sisters know she's alive.

This shit with Chanel is really fucking up my mental. I've been off my square in the streets and that ain't good for business. I've even went so far as to hire a private detective. He couldn't even find her and he was supposed to be the best in the business. A part of me wondered if she had hurt herself and was in a morgue somewhere. Her credit or debit cards hadn't been used. Her cell phone had no activity. The other part of me knew she would never kill herself. I hurt her to the core with this Samina shit. The bad part about it was that she really worked for me. I let her suck the D from time to time but that was it. We met up at the hotel every week for me to collect my money and for her to re-up.

I should have just kept shit one hundred with her instead of disrespecting her and telling her we were over. I guess I just thought she would leave for a couple of days and all would be forgiven. She tricked my ass good this time. Not knowing where she could be had me all in my feelings. I didn't know if I would be able to live with myself.

I drove the city checking the traps and making sure niggas was handling their business. I was so lost in my thoughts that I almost ran a stop sign and hit a crack head.

"What the fuck? Pay attention, nigga," the lady said as she hit the top of my Benz.

I jumped out ready to beat this lady ass until I locked eyes with the woman who birthed and abandoned me and King. It was Trixie, our long lost mother, and she looked worse than Alfre Woodard in the movie *Holiday Heart*.

"Nassie, baby is that you."

A pain shot through my heart as I heard her call me the pet name she had given me. Tears streamed down my face as she wrapped her arms around my neck and hugged me. She smelled horrible. I gently removed her arms from around me and stared at her.

"Get in the car. You need to get cleaned up."

She got inside the car and we drove back to my house. While she was in the tub, I fixed her something to eat. I was glad Chanel still had clothes in the crib. She looked as if she hadn't eaten in months. I made sure to call King and let him know she was at my crib. He had some choice words for her leaving us and some choice words for me picking her up. I don't know why I picked her up. I guess when I saw her, I was still the little boy who sat in the window waiting for his mother to return home.

My cell phone chimed alerted me that I had a message. The messages were from the private detective. I clicked on the message and it opened up. I had to take a double take because it was Chanel and her stomach was huge. He had an address for her as well. I couldn't believe she had been in Georgia all this time. The sight of her protruding belly enraged me to the point where I started breaking shit. I didn't even know King and Gucci had come inside the crib until I heard her calling my name and felt King grabbing on me

"What the fuck is wrong with you, lil bro?" King said as he

pushed me out of the patio door.

"Chanel is what the fuck is wrong with me. You remember I told you I hired a private detective, right? Look at this shit here."

I showed him the pictures of Chanel that the guy had sent me. I watched his reaction at the sight of her stomach. He looked over his shoulder to make sure Gucci wasn't in earshot.

"Do you think Gucci and Dior knew where she has been all this time?" I had to ask because they are thick as thieves. He shook his head no.

"I doubt it. They recently filed a missing person's report. Do you think it's your seed?"

"That's all me."

"What are you going to do?"

"I'm going to Atlanta and drag her ass back home. Don't tell Gucci. I can't believe that she would keep my seed away from me. I know that I fucked us up but she's dead wrong for not telling me she was pregnant."

"I won't say shit. What the fuck are you going to do with your crack head ass mother? I'm not fucking with her deadbeat ass until she gets clean.

"Damn, I forgot about her ass that quickly."

We both walked back in the house and our mother and Gucci were in the kitchen finishing up the meal I started.

"Oh my God. Look at my baby, King."

My mother walked towards King and wrapped her arms around him and he pried her arms from around him.

"Come on, you're going to the rehab right now. I suggest you finish the program in its entirety. If you don't. It would be on your best interest to never come around us again.

King grabbed Trixie and led her out the door. There was nothing I could say because I totally agreed with him. Plus, I had other shit on my plate at the moment. I headed to my room and lay across the bed. I couldn't stop staring at the picture of Chanel. I hadn't realized how much I missed her until I seen the picture. I opened up my laptop and booked a redeye flight to Georgia. I was about to snatch her ass up and bring her ass back home. That was my fucking word.

CHAPTER 12 - King Carter

Comes To the Light

I had no words for my mother. I couldn't even look at her as we drove to the Women's Treatment Center. I didn't care if I was acting mean to her. Her feelings didn't mean a damn thing to me because she didn't care about her sons feelings when she walked out the door on us. It was fucked up but I hated my mother. She knew it too.

Gucci made small talk with her the entire ride. She was telling her all about Imani. I wasn't cool with that shit. She didn't deserve to know anything about her granddaughter. She lost that privilege a long time ago. When we arrived at the rehab, Gucci gave her our numbers and some money. I wasn't giving her shit. She had to prove that she wanted to be in our lives. We walked her inside and talked to her counselors for about an hour and we headed home.

"Do you want to talk about it?" Gucci said as she sat next to me on the couch in my man cave.

"Not really."

"Baby, I think you should talk about it. You're holding all your emotions inside and that is not good."

"Shut the fuck up! I said I didn't want to talk about it."

I threw the glass I was holding against the wall. I grabbed my keys and walked out of the house. I needed to get out of the house for a little while to clear my head. I decided to head to Gentlemen's Paradise. I had Dutch meet me up there so that we could have a couple of drinks and chill.

As soon as I arrived at the club, I wanted to turn right back around. Samaya was the first person I saw. This was strip club for men. I didn't understand why her and her whack ass crew was in there. I'm starting to believe those hoes are carpet munchers. I walked right past her and joined Dutch at the bar.

"What's good, my nigga?" I asked as we dapped each other up.

"Shit. I talked to Nasir. He just took flight. I hope he don't go down there wilding. The last thing we need is him to get locked up out of state."

"I hope Chanel just come back with his ass. They're probably humbugging right now. We both laughed because we knew just how crazy they could get.

"You're acting funny, King," Samaya whispered in my ear and grabbed my dick at the same time.

"I'm not in the mood for your shit today, Maya. Get the fuck away from me before I embarrass your ass in here." I roughly pushed her away from me.

"All of sudden you're trying to be faithful to that lame bitch. Don't forget I'm the one that grind hard for you in these streets because that bitch thinks she's too good. You're always knee deep in this pussy so stop fronting on me." She muffed me upside my head. Before I knew it, I had my hands wrapped around her throat trying to squeeze the life out of her.

"You better watch your mouth bitch! I'll snap your mother-fucking neck. Did you forget who I am? Say my fucking name. I think you forgot who you're fucking with."

"King," she managed to say with what little breath she had.

"Now get the fuck away from me and act like the peasant bitch you are. Consider your ass cancelled since you like running off at the mouth." I slapped her so hard she hit the floor. Her thot ass friends all ran to her and helped her up.

"Chill out, bro," Dutch said as he grabbed me because he knew I wanted to beat her ass.

"I'm good. That bitch been trying my patience since I made shit official with G. I shouldn't have let her suck my dick back in the ninth grade. She has been a pain in my ass ever since."

"You and Nasir fucked up when ya'll started letting them hoes do drug runs. Now they know too much shit. I have a feeling they are going to be bad for business."

"I wish that bitch would. I'll break her fucking neck and throw that bitch in Lake Michigan."

We sat and drank a couple of more shots and headed out. The next day was the first of the month so I had to be out bright and early make sure all the traps were filled with product and my cash flow was on point.

I knew that I needed to tell Gucci about the incident with Samaya. The last thing I needed was for shit to get back to her from another source. We had been good since she moved in and I wanted to keep that way. I hadn't been with Samaya like that since I made shit official. I had just purchased my baby a ring. Tahari and Dior had been helping with all the preparations. Samaya had another thing coming if she thought that she was going to come between me and my baby.

Imani and Gucci was asleep on the couch when I walked into the house. I picked up Imani and carried her to her room. I tucked her in and headed back to wake up Gucci but she had already got up and climbed in bed. I could tell she was still pissed about earlier. I took a quick shower and climbed in bed with her.

"You sleep, G? I need to holla at you about something."

"Leave me alone King."

She pulled the covers over her head. I pulled them from over her head. She sat straight up and stared at me.

"I'm sorry about earlier. I was wrong for spazzing out on you like that. Do you forgive me?" I grabbed her chin and kissed her on the lips.

"Of course I forgive you. Now what do you want to talk about? It's late and I have a date with Imani tomorrow. You already know she wakes up bright eyes and bushy tailed."

"I had to lay hands on the bitch Samaya at the club. Before you go off, hear me out. She started talking reckless about us messing around. I can assure you since we've been together officially, I haven't even entertained the thought of another female.

"Is that all? I expect for her to say shit like that because I know she wants you and she will do whatever she can to break us up. I'm not entertaining that delusional bitch."

"I'm glad to hear that but there's something else. Samaya and Samina have been doing drug runs for us. I fucked up by sleeping with the bitch from time to time and now she's getting reckless. I just wanted to let you know about all the bullshit."

"So, that bitch has been getting money with you all this time. No wonder she's so disrespectful to me. You have given her the ammunition to play me out in public because she has one up on me. That's why she always talking shit. I'm not allowed to put in work beside you but your side bitch can?"

"You're my fucking wife. You would never be out in the streets hustling. That's my job. All you need to do is raise our daughter and spend my money. I was wrong for never telling you. You don't have anything to worry about. I deaded that shit. She will no longer do drug runs for us. That's my word, G."

"If you think it's that easy, you're stupider than I thought. I can't believe you right now."

Gucci laid down and turned her back to me. I knew she would be pissed. I'm just glad she knows I'm not cheating on her. I need to get the word out to my people that she and her buzzard ass friends are not to step foot in or around my traps. I hate to admit it but I know Samaya is about to turn all the way up.

Chapter 13 - Gucci

Hating Ass Bitches

Imani and I walked around the mall putting a dent in King's black card. I deserved any fucking thing I wanted after finding out about him letting Samaya do drug runs for him. King had no business letting her get money with him. It's the principle of it all. King just better hope all ties are severed between them immediately.

Lately, I've been so lonely without my sisters. Dior hasn't been in the best of moods and I don't know why. Chanel is still missing and we have no idea where she could be. The worst part is our mother acts as if she doesn't even care. I wanted to smack the shit out of her when she said that Chanel was somewhere licking her wounds. Her ass calls and checks on Nasir more than she calls the police station to see if they have any leads. I tried to get Dior to come to the mall with me but her ass just wants to stay in the house. I don't know what's going on with her and Dutch but something isn't right. I have every intention on finding out what the hell is going on.

"Mommy, I want my nails to be pink and lime green," Imani said as she was picking out her colors for her nails. She was such a little diva.

"Just get pink and next week you can do lime green. Daddy, doesn't like it when you get all of those colors."

She was rolling her eyes at me but she wouldn't dare do that with King. The nail salon inside the mall was crowded and I really didn't want to wait.

"Let's go get something to eat, baby girl. It's too crowded. We can go to the nail shop closer to home."

I grabbed her hand and we headed out the door and towards

the food court. I spotted Samaya and some more girls walking in my direction. We locked eyes and I knew she was about to try me. I reached inside my purse for my phone and realized I left it in the car on the charger. For some reason I felt like this bitch wanted to fight or something. I didn't care about fighting. I just didn't want to do it while my daughter was with me.

"I swear to God I can't stand this bitch," Samaya said as she blocked my path.

"You better get your Amazon looking ass out of my fucking way. As you can see, I have my daughter with me. I really don't have time to entertain your delusional ass." I tried to walk past her but the girls that she was with surrounded me and my daughter.

"There ain't shit delusional about me. If you think you're the only one in King's life, then your delusional. I've been around for years and I'm not going anywhere."

"You've been around all these years and what do you have to show for it? A drug run here, a dick in your mouth there. Bitch get you a life and stop trying to live mine. That shit is pathetic."

"Ohh Mommy, you said bad words." For a quick second I forgot my daughter was with me.

"You know what; I have my daughter with me. We'll see each other again. Mommy's sorry for saying bad words."

I grabbed her hand and pushed passed Samaya and her friends. A punch to the back of my head instantly made me turn around and start swinging. I had a death grip on one of the girls and was kicking her ass. I felt punches and kicks raining down all over my body. The sound of my baby crying made me cry. I couldn't believe these hoes were jumping on me while I had my baby with me.

They were trying their best to get me down on the ground but I wasn't going down that easily. I was fighting to the death and my daughter's cries kept me going. I felt a stinging sensation across my chest. The next thing I knew, I was hit in my face with something hard. I fell to the floor and the bitches continued to stomp me. I couldn't believe no one helped me out. They just stood around videotaping the shit. Security finally arrived. I was starting to black out. My eyes were swollen so I couldn't really see. I knew my baby was on the floor next to me. I couldn't do anything but cry as I heard her screaming and hollering.

"Oh my God! Somebody calls the ambulance. All you stupid motherfuckers standing around watching this shit. Come on baby girl. It's okay. Mommy's okay." I heard a lady with the sweetest voice calming Imani down. I don't remember anything after that because I lost consciousness.

Chapter 14-Chanel

Facing The Music

I've been so happy since I left Chicago because I have a peace of mind. I miss Chanel, Dior, and my niece. It's sad but my mother hasn't even crossed my mind. I know she's back home all up in Nasir's ass. My only regret I have is leaving and not reaching out to my sisters. I hope they understand my reasons behind what I did.

After a month of being here in Georgia, I found a great job as a medical receptionist at the local hospital and a nice condo. I stopped drinking cold turkey because I found out I was two months pregnant about a week after I arrived here. I had been so stressed that I never realized that I had missed my periods.

I can't believe the liquor didn't make me sick. I've been stressed because I keep thinking my liquor intake will affect my son. The doctor has assured me the baby will be fine. I'm almost nine months pregnant and Nasir doesn't even know he has a son on the way. I feel so bad about not telling him. I decided not to tell anyone for the sake of my heart and my mind. They would have tried to convince me to go back to Chicago. I would be lying if I said I didn't miss Nasir. I miss him so much. Sometimes I lie in bed and wonder if he even misses me or if I ever cross his mind from time to time.

****

As I walked out of my job, I couldn't wait to get home and put my feet up. My feet were swollen and my back was killing me. I had been having lower back pains all week and I was starting to get scared like I was going to go in labor early. Those thoughts made me realize that I had no one to take me to the hospital or be in the delivery room with me when I gave birth to my son. I was seriously rethinking this whole situation. I made it up in my mind that when I made it home, I was going to call my sisters and let them know everything.

My apartment was on the second floor and the stairs were getting harder to climb. Plus, I had to pee. It took me about five minutes to wobble up the stairs. Finally, I made it up to my door and went in with my key. I dropped everything and took off towards the bathroom. I ran dead smack into Nasir coming out of the bathroom.

"What the fuck are you doing here?" I was looking like a deer in headlights. The look on his face told me he was angry. I was so damn scared I pissed all over myself.

"Get your shit and let's go!" He grabbed my arm and yanked me. I snatched away from him.

"I'm not going anywhere with you. Go find that bitch Samina. I'm good."

I folded my hands across my chest and stood there. Nasir moved so close to me his breath was tickling my nose.

"I don't have time for that bullshit you talking about. You up and disappeared. Got me and your family worried sick about your ass, Putting out missing person's reports, Hiring private detectives to find you, and Hoping your ass ain't dead somewhere. Not to mention your ass is pregnant. Tell me this; were you ever going to let me know I had a child?" I could see the hurt in his eyes but so what! I was hurting too.

"Please, Nasir. Miss me with the 'I give a damn about you' speech. If you cared about me so much, you never would have put me out of our home. You never would have disrespected me in front of our friends and family. You wouldn't have been cheating on me. I can't believe you let that nasty bitch suck your dick in the bathroom like I wasn't even in the building. I'm so over this shit with you. Now get the fuck out of my way so I can take a shower."

I pushed his ass to the side, went into the bathroom, and locked it behind me. I had so many emotions going on inside of me. I was happy to see him and I was mad because he was here. I had found my happy place and he was here to fuck it up. I cried the entire time I showered. I stayed in the bathroom as long as I could. I wrapped myself up in a towel and got ready to face the music.

When I walked into my bedroom, I couldn't believe Nasir was actually packing my clothes. He looked good as fuck and I couldn't help but lick my lips at all his sexiness. His dreads had gotten longer since the last time I seen him. His skin was still the perfect shade of brown. The Chap Stick on his lips glistened as he moved around the room.

"Why are you touching my things?" I had a devilish grin on my face as I spoke.

"Cut the bullshit. Get dressed right motherfucking now. You're going home. End of fucking discussion. We can do this the easy way or the hard way."

"What's the hard way?" I was in shock as he pulled a nine from his waist.

"I'm taking you and my seed back home by any means necessary."

I was mad and turned on at the same time. Nasir walked towards me and pulled me into his embrace.

"I'm sorry, baby. I missed you so much. I know I fucked up. The last thing I ever wanted to do was hurt you. Now you're carrying my seed and that shit means the world to me. Please come home and let's work this shit out. I want my family."

Nasir removed the towel from around my body and got down on his knees. He placed soft kisses on my stomach. His touch made my body shiver and my son kick. He leaned me against the door and lifted my leg up on his shoulder. He placed soft kisses on my inner thighs. I started to breathe harder as the anticipation of him making love to my pussy set in. The moment his tongue came in contact with my clit, I let out the loudest moan. I knew my neighbors heard me. I pulled his head in closer and wrapped his dreads around my hands. I wanted to feed him all of me.

"Turn around," Nasir commanded and I complied. He spread my legs apart and placed my arms flat against the door. The sound of him unbuckling his belt had me nervous. It had been a minute since I felt him inside of me. He was well endowed so I was ready for the pain and the pleasure that was sure to follow. He rammed is dick inside of me and began to slide in and out me carefully.

"Damn! I missed you so much," Nasir moaned in pleasure. I could feel him biting and sucking all over my neck.

"Mmmm! I missed you too." I hated to admit it but I did. Plus, that good dick he was giving me had me in another damn zone.

"You gon' bring that ass home."

"Yessss!"

Nasir was hitting my G-Spot each and every time he thrusted in and out of me, I was trying my best not to answer but Nasir was relentless and showing my pussy no mercy. At that moment, I would have said yes to anything.

We both came at the same time and his cell phone started ringing. He looked at it answered. I walked out of the room and went to clean myself up. When I walked back in the room, his facial expression was scary.

"I told you I'm coming home. Your ass don't have to look like that." I started putting on my clothes and grabbing my important information.

"Gucci is in the hospital. We need to get back to the Chi immediately."

"What's wrong with my sister? Is she okay?"

"King didn't go into details. Let's grab your luggage and go. We'll hire a moving company to come get everything else."

I really wasn't hearing anything Nasir was saying. My son was kicking up the storm. He knew his mommy was upset. As I sat on the airplane, my mind was going into overdrive thinking about my sister and what was going on. Besides that, thoughts of Nasir and Samina were heavy on my mind. He never responded when I brought up the fact that he was cheating on me. I hope he doesn't think we're good just because he laid that good pipe to my ass. He still has some explaining to do. That shit will have to wait until later. Right now, my main focus is my sister.

Chapter 15 - King

Someone Has to Pay

When I received the phone call from a stranger telling me what had happened, I didn't know what to do. I was thankful that Imani knew my phone number by heart. She gave the lady my number and then she told me what had happened. My mind was on a thousand as I headed to the hospital. I made sure to call the family so that they could meet me up there. As I walked inside the hospital, I found Imani with the woman who called me. I took Imani off of her lap and she wrapped her arms around me so tight. I could tell my baby was scared.

"Thank you so much for calling me."

"No problem. Please keep my number and let me know that she is okay. Someone should be out shortly to update you. I'm going to leave know so that you and your family could be together. See you later, Imani." She kissed her on the jaw and left. I was so thankful to the lady. As soon as I called her, I definitely was going to look out for her.

"Are you okay, Daddy's baby?"

"The mean ladies hurt Mommy. They wouldn't let us walk past."

She laid her head on my shoulders and I clenched my jaw. Angry wasn't even the word to describe how I was feeling. That was some coward shit they pulled. I couldn't wait to find out who had did this to her.

"Oh my God! Where is my baby at, King?"

"Calm down, Candy. She's in the back. I haven't heard anything yet."

"Mommy was bleeding, Grandma." Imani made tears come to my eyes as she said that. I had no idea Gucci was bleeding.

"Come on baby. Let's go get some candy from the vending machine."

Candy took Imani out of my arms and I walked up to the nurses' station to get some information on Gucci. I got a text message from Thug calling an emergency meeting. I would have to get back to him once I knew my baby was okay. I was becoming impatient as hell. After waiting a couple of more minutes a doctor came out looking for us.

"Right here. I'm her husband." We shook hands and I really didn't like the expression on his face.

"Ms. Lennox is stabilized now. When she came in, she had a laceration across her chest and one to her head from a razor blade. She needed twenty-five staples to close the wound. We also had to put ten staples in her head. Ms. Lennox also has a concussion and a broken arm. All of her injuries should heal perfectly fine. I want to keep her overnight since she has a concussion. I'll release her first thing in the morning."

"Thanks, Doc. Can I go back and see her know?"

"Yes, you can."

Candy and Imani had made it back and we all walked back to see her. When we walked into the room, Gucci was sitting there staring off into space. Imani jumped out of her grandma's arms and climbed into bed with Gucci. I hated that she had scratches and bruises all over her face. I could even see where the bitches had pulled her hair out.

"I'm okay, momma's baby." Gucci kissed her all over her face. I could tell that she was in pain by the way she was wincing.

"I'm so glad you're okay. I'm going to take Imani home with me. She has been through a lot today and she needs to sleep. I'll be here bright and early to pick you up when you're released. I love you Gucci."

Candy hugged and kissed Gucci. It surprised me because I have never seen her show her daughters any type of affection. Gucci was surprised too. Once they left, I pulled a chair up close to her bed and held on tight to her hand.

"Who did this shit to you?" I asked as I kissed her on the lips and she grabbed the sides of my face and kissed me back.

"I don't know who the bitches were, King. My head is really hurting right now. All I want to do is sleep. You can go home. I'll see you in the morning."

I knew that Gucci was lying through her teeth. There was no way she had no idea who did this to her. I was so mad at her. I had to leave the hospital before I cursed her ass out.

"Do you want me to get you anything before I leave?"

"I'm good. I'll see you in the morning."

We kissed one last time and I left the hospital. Heated wasn't even the word. How could Gucci not want to tell me who the fuck did this to her? I ran into Dutch and Dior on my way out of the hospital.

"Please tell me my sister is okay." Dior had tears in her eyes.

"She's fine. You should go up there and sit with her. Maybe she will tell you who the fuck did this to her because she won't tell me shit."

"She's probably just upset. You know how stubborn Gucci can be."

"Hey ya'll," a familiar voice said. We all turned around to see Nasir and Chanel standing there. She was big as a damn house.

"Really bitch? This is how you're doing it now?" Dior said.

She walked away and went into the hospital. Chanel was hurt by Dior's actions. They would have to deal with that shit amongst themselves. I had bigger shit to deal with.

"Baby, just go inside and see what's good with Gucci. It will give ya'll time to catch up. Call me when you're ready to go home." Chanel hesitated but she went inside the hospital.

"Come roll with me. Thug called an emergency meeting with us. It has to be some shit going on. You know he never calls a meeting at the last minute. I'll deal with this Gucci situation later."

We all jumped in our cars and made our way over to Thug's. I couldn't help but wonder what the fuck was going on.

Chapter 16 - Thug

Unpaid Debts

When I took over the Santarelli Family I also inherited a lot of unpaid debts that were now owed to me. I hadn't realized how much I had took on until I received all of the paperwork from my grandfather's attorney. There were endless deeds to properties all over the fucking world. I put Tahari, Ta'jay, Keesha, Khia, and Barbie in charge of the properties across the city. The girls needed something to do. I wanted them to get out and get their feet wet in real estate. The majority of the properties were fronts for our drug trafficking organization so they would make shit look legit and we wouldn't have to deal with the police breathing down our necks.

Ta-Baby has taken on her role as mob wife just like I knew she would. I never doubted her. Life is a lot better for us now. Our relationship is stronger than ever. We make sure to never go to bed mad. We've come too far to beef with each other. Plus, a happy wife is a happy life. The last thing I need to do is get on my wife bad side. She isn't taking any shit and I'm not playing any games with her.

I love spending time with my kids. I really missed them being babies. Now they are growing up right before my eyes. They can't get enough of their daddy. Tahari hates it because we never really have any alone time. All she wants to do is keep a nigga on his back. Her sex drive is crazy. I never been the one to tap out but lately she's been having a nigga wore the fuck out.

"Are you busy, Ka'Jaire? I need to talk to you about something." Ta-Baby came into my conference room wearing a pair of white leggings and a tank top.

"I'm never too busy for you, Ma. I did just call a meeting with the crew. Some serious shit has been brought to my attention and I need to get to the bottom of the shit." I kissed her on the lips and pulled her on my lap.

"It's about to be our five year anniversary and we never really got around to renewing our vows. Since we own that island in Cabo, I was thinking we should do a couples' retreat and we renew our vows there. I already looked into it and there are seven Villas on the island. That is more than enough room for everybody."

"Damn, I can't believe we've been together for five years already. Time flies fast as hell. I love you Ta-Baby. We can do whatever you like, Ma. Just make all the arrangements. I'll holla at the crew. Not everybody will be able to go. Somebody has to stay back and hold down shit here."

"I already took care of that. Markese, Rahmeek, Killa, and Boogie will all stay back and run shit in the streets. Aja, Trish, Stacy, and Nisa will make sure the properties stay running properly. King and his crew need a getaway. They have been doing numbers in the streets."

"That's why I love you, Ma. You always have everything under control. Let me holla at them when they come to the meeting and let them know the game plan. Once they all confirm, we can start booking flights."

"Okay, baby," Tahari said as she started placing kisses all over my face and unbuckling my belt at the same time.

I couldn't do shit but shake my head. I stood up so that she could pull my pants down. Once she released my dick, she placed it in her mouth and began to make mad passionate love to it. After all these years, she still stands to be the coldest when it comes to giving a nigga head. I couldn't help but grab her head and roughly pump her mouth. She was humming, moaning, slurping, sucking, and gagging all at the same time. She was giving me that real sloppy toppy million-dollar mouth that I love so much. I felt my nut build up and I released it all in her mouth. She swallowed each and every drop. She stood up smiling and wiping her mouth with the back of her hand.

"Hurry up with this meeting. I want some of that dick. I'll be waited on you naked." She walked out of the room. I had to light a blunt and drink some Red Bull. I needed all the energy in the world. I knew Tahari was trying to pull an all-nighter on my ass.

****

"It's about time ya'll got here. What the fuck took you so long?" I asked as King, Nasir, and Dutch walked into the conference room. Sarge, Malik, Quaadir, and Dro had already arrived.

"Sorry about that. We were at the hospital with Gucci. Some bitches jumped her at the mall while she had my daughter."

King looked upset and it was understandable but I had told them a long time ago to stop letting their ladies go out without security detail. They aren't little niggas anymore selling packs. They're moving weight, making bands, and bodying motherfuckers left and right.

"Gucci cool, lil bro?" Malik asked as he lit a blunt.

"She has a concussion, a broken arm, and needed twenty five fucking staples across her chest from being slashed. I'm fucked up because she won't tell me who did the shit to her."

"You already know who did that shit, King. There is nothing like a woman scorned. Samaya and that ugly ass crew of hers did that shit to her. I heard about what happened at Gentlemen's Paradise. That bitch has been all on Facebook talking shit about you and your girl. You need to tighten up. That Facebook shit ain't no joke. I almost lost Tahari over that shit."

"Damn right, you did. Is Gucci okay? I just got off the phone with Barbie and she told me about that bullshit them hoes pulled. The days of them hoes getting money is over. I don't know why you motherfuckers mix business with pleasure. This is the shit that happens."

Tahari just came in the conference room without knocking. She's Boss Lady and all but she knows to never come in their when we're conducting business. Tahari knew that bursting inside the conference room during a meeting was way out of line. I stared at her and let her know to get the fuck out of the room.

"I already cut the bitch off, Boss Lady. That was the first thing I did after I choked her ass up at the club."

King was pissed off and he should be. I'm not giving him any orders on what to do. Bitches come with the territory. I'm going to fall back and let him handle this shit. By the look in his eyes, I already know what it is.

"Tahari, close the door on your way out."

She rolled her eyes and slammed the door. I didn't give a fuck. I definitely was going to get at her ass about her behavior. She is starting to take this Boss Lady shit too fucking far. She forgot who the motherfucking boss is.

"Let's get down to why I called ya'll here. This morning I was going through some of the paperwork from the attorney and came across this." I handed them some paperwork and pictures and they passed it around the table.

"I know you're wondering who the fuck dude is in the picture. That is the infamous Sincere "Ox" Lennox, long thought to have been dead but that motherfucker is very much alive. He ran off with thirty million dollars worth of product and cash from Vito back in the day. The nigga faked his death and is back on the scene because he thinks the Santerelli Family has all been eliminated. Everyone at this table knows I don't give a fuck about any debt that's owed to them. The shit has nothing to do with me or our organization. That was until he stepped inside Gentlemen's Paradise talking reckless about how the streets of Chicago belonged to him and how he would off any nigga that stepped in his way. There can be only one King of the Chi and from what I hear about this nigga, he was real ruthless and dirty back in the day. It's a new day and he ain't ready for what the streets has for his ass. Especially, since we run these motherfucking streets. Ya'll already know what it is." I leaned back in my chair and knocked back a shot of Remy waiting for everyone's response.

"Fuck my life," King said as he pushed the pictures back. I looked at Nasir and Dutch. They all wore the same expression as King.

"That's Gucci and her sisters father. They think that nigga dead."

"Here comes the bullshit," Malik spoke up as he opened the

fifth of Remy and poured himself a shot.

"It's up to you niggas how you want to handle shit as far as your ladies go. As far as the money and this organization, the nigga has to go. We won't move on his ass right away because of the situation that you all have been put in. Don't say anything to them about their father being alive."

"I'm ten steps ahead of you. I had no intention on saying shit anyway. I'm wondering how the nigga just disappeared on them and popped back up without even getting at them. That shit has my antennas so far up, it's crazy."

"I'm with you, King. That motherfucker up to no good," Nasir said and Dutch nodded his head in agreement.

For the rest of the night, we sat back discussed business and the trip that Tahari planned. They all agreed to go. I was glad because we needed a break from business for a minute. I just wanted to chill back with my crew and celebrate with my crazy ass wife.

Chapter 17 - Gucci

Dirty Laundry

I really wasn't in the mood to talk to anyone, not even Chanel and Dior. Ever since they walked into my hospital room, they have been arguing about Chanel being pregnant and disappearing on us. I wanted answers as well but right now, the focus should be on me and how we're going to get these bitches back.

"Would ya'll shut the fuck up!" I screamed so loud and it hurt my head. I wanted to grip the sides of my head until the pain subsided but one of my fucking arms was broke. I guess I got their attention because both of them stop talking.

"Sorry, G. Are you okay?" Dior said as she sat in the chair next to my bed. Chanel wobbled her ass over and sat on the bed.

"I'm good. I'm just in a lot of pain. I can't believe them bitches jumped on me while I had Imani with me." Tears escaped from my eyes as I could hear my baby crying at the top of her lungs.

"Wait a minute, this happened while you had my niece with you?"

"So, who did it? King can handle those bitches," Chanel said as she rubbed her stomach.

"Do ya'll ever get tired of our niggas handling shit for us? That's why I'm laid up in here now. King holds me down but I have to start holding my own. Both of you need to start doing the same. That's why these hoes be stepping to us. We need to start making examples out of these bitches. A message needs to be sent that we're not to be fucked with. I don't know about ya'll but the days of me sitting back on my looking pretty while King puts in work are over. I'm shooting first and not asking any questions. As soon as I heal and you drop that load, we're putting in work. Let me know now if ya'll ain't with it. I'll get that hoe Samaya and them bitches by myself."

"Don't ever say nothing like that to us again. You already know we're riding with you. I totally agree with everything you said," Dior said as she stood up and kissed me on the forehead.

"I should have known those bitches were behind this shit."

"Calm down, Chanel. You're going to upset my niece or nephew and those bitches aren't worth it. They've done enough damage."

"It's a boy."

I could see it in Chanel's eyes that she was happy about giving birth. I also could see that Dior wouldn't look at her stomach or touch it like I was doing. She was in another world as Chanel and I discussed names. The situation had depressed her and I didn't understand why because she's the one who always said she didn't want to kids.

Chanel and Dior stayed until visiting hours were over. While they were there, we talked about how we were going to get those bitches back. We never spoke about Chanel leaving or Dior's shitty mood. I wasn't going to press the issue. They would talk about it when they were ready.

I knew that King was upset with me for not telling him who jumped. I have intentions on dealing with situation my way. I didn't want King trying to get payback for me. I needed to do it for myself.

I was so happy the next day when I was released. I had been calling King since he left the hospital yesterday. He never answered my calls. I just kept getting his voicemail. That was confirmation that he was mad at my ass. I just called a cab because I wanted to get to the mall and get my car before it was towed. The cab arrived and we headed over to the mall.

My car was destroyed. The windows were busted out. All the tires had been flattened. Someone slashed my interior to shreds. It had so many dents in it. I was livid. King just brought me this Benz and it was my baby. Side bitches will do anything to get a niggas attention. Side bitches should always play the background and shut the fuck up. I just don't understand why this bitch likes fucking with me. Samaya wants my life so bad that she is willing to do anything to have it. Too bad that she will never know what it feels like to be King's queen. I hold that title and I stand to be the coldest in my position.

I had the cab driver take me straight home. After seeing my car my head started hurting again.

"Why you didn't call anyone to come and get you? You're in no condition to be driving," my mother said as she grabbed my arm and led me to the couch. I was in no mood for this Mother Theresa role she had been playing lately. It was creeping me the hell out. She showed no one affection like this but Imani.

"I called a cab because I couldn't get in contact with King. Is he here?"

"No. He left as soon as I came. He and Nasir went to pick their mother up from the rehab. She's going to stay here for the weekend. I decided to cook lunch for everybody, fried chicken and some potato salad."

"Good, I'm hungry as hell. Where is Imani?"

"She's upstairs in your room watching Doc McStuffins. She will be so glad you're home. That shit really upset her." As my mother spoke, I turned around and headed upstairs to see my baby. I could only imagine how she is feeling.

"Hey Mommy! Is your boo-boo okay?" She felt my head and kissed me on the jaw at the same time.

"Yes. It's just fine now that I got all that sweet sugar."

We hugged and kissed for a minute then I got in the tub. I just wanted to soak all the bullshit away. I tried my best not to get my cast wet. My chest started to hurt so I got out so that I could take some pain medicine. I looked in the mirror at my chest and I cringed. The staples were so ugly. I knew there would be an ugly scar. A bitch definitely was paying for some plastic surgery. The sound of arguing downstairs made me get dressed and rush back downstairs.

"I can't believe you, Chanel. How could you just leave and not say anything? We were worried sick about you." My mother and Chanel were in a shouting match and I wasn't in the mood for the shit.

"Since when did you ever worry about anybody?"

"You better watch your motherfucking mouth, Chanel, before I hit you in it." I watched my mother walk closer to Chanel. I just knew she was about to about to pop her. They used to actually fist fight when we were younger.

I advise you to get out of my face. If you hit me, I'm hitting your ass back." Chanel walked away and sat on the couch.

"You're one disrespectful ass little bitch. Lately, all of you have really been showing your asses. Please don't forget that I will knock your fucking teeth down your throat. Dior don't think I forgot that you haven't been answering my calls or your door for me. I have the right mind to slap fire from your ass too. I know you're in pain, Gucci, but I haven't forgotten about your smart ass mouth either. You bitches better adjust your fucking attitudes before I do it for you. You hoes have gotten grown and think it's okay to disrespect me."

We all just stood there looking at her because this was nothing new. Even as little girls, we were all types of bitches and hoes. She wanted respect when she never respected us. She kept food on the table, clothes on our back, and a roof over our head. That was it. This lady truly had issues and she was about to get put out of my house.

"Don't start with me. I'm going through a lot right now," Dior cried.

"What could you possibly be going through? As a matter fact, what could possibly be going on with any of you? You have the best men in the world taking care of you and giving you a great life but all ya'll do is bitch and moan about everything. Ya'll are so fucking weak and pathetic."

"Oh hell no. You got to get the fuck out of my house. You will not stand here and disrespect me in my house. You have no idea what we go through because your head is too far up our niggas ass. Can we please get some love, support, and affection from you For once? I just got my ass whooped by one of King's side bitches. You're sadly mistaken if you think he is a saint. King cheats on me all the time."

Now Chanel was crying. "I left because I caught Nasir letting some bitch suck his dick in the club. Then he turned around and put me the fuck out of our house like I wasn't shit. I found I was pregnant a little after I went down there. Not everything is about you like you try to make it out to be. I'm pregnant with my first child and you don't even care."

"I just suffered a miscarriage at the hands of the man that is supposed to love me. My first baby was beat out of me and I don't know how to deal with it."

At this point Dior was crying hysterically. Chanel and I ran to her side to comfort her. Now I understand why she has been so distant lately. Our mother just stood there looking like the fool she was.

"So, that's how we're doing it now? We're just airing our fucking dirty laundry."

I looked up and Dutch was standing there with steam coming from his ears. I could also tell he was embarrassed that we knew what was going on with them. King, Nasir, and their mother were also standing in the foyer. I wasn't sure if they heard what had been said.

"Didn't I tell you if we ever crossed paths, I was beating your ass. My mother charged Trixie and they began to fight. Trixie was no match for Candy. She was tagging her ass.

"Let her go Ma! I screamed as I pried her hands from around Trixie's throat.

"Break this shit up! Candy, you have to get out. Disrespecting my house. What were you thinking by attacking my mother?" King was livid. If she weren't my mother, he probably would have shot her by now.

"This bitch is the reason why my man is dead now. With her conniving ass. I don't know why Ox even gave your ugly ass a second thought."

"Bitch please. Ox wasn't your man. He was my man and everybody else's too. I see your ass still live on Fantasy Island. Get it through your head, Candy, we were his hoes. We shared the dick, at the same time on several occasions. The only difference was you had three children for him. Don't forget I know all about your past. I advise you to pipe down before it be some more fights up in here."

I looked at my mother trying to get an inkling as to what Trixie was talking about. Whatever she meant had my mother quiet as a fucking church mouse. We all stood around trying to process what the hell just happened.

"Shut up, Trixie! It's not going to be any more fights in my shit!" King said.

"Don't worry about me, you crack head bitch. Worry about who the father of your kids is. I definitely know who fathered mine." Candy started grabbing her things and headed towards the door.

"That's your problem, bitch. You think you know every fucking thing. The father of my children is Mike Jordan. Does the name ring a bell?"

Trixie was grinning like the Cheshire Cat. Candy just shook her head and walked out the door. It was crazy that they were both standing in front of their children revealing secrets as if they wouldn't affect us. Who would have thought our mothers were hoes for the same pimp. This some Jerry Springer bullshit.

"Ya'll really in here doing all this while my daughter in here. Gucci bring your ass upstairs. I need to holla at you real quick."

"About what?"

"Don't make me embarrass your motherfucking ass! Let's go now."

I didn't understand why he was so mad at me. It wasn't my fault our mothers got into a fight. I was upset as well. All I could do was think about Dior. I have never seen her so upset. I couldn't believe Dutch had did that to her. He always had a temper. I just didn't know it was that bad.

"All this time you knew who our father was and you just abandoned us. That's fucked up but I'm not surprised. Let's go, Chanel."

Nasir helped Chanel up and they walked out of the house. Dutch grabbed Dior and they also left. Trixie was now sitting on the couch playing with Imani. I exhaled and made my way up-stairs to see what King was so mad about. If anything, I should be mad at his black ass.

I walked in the room. He was sitting on the bed smoking a blunt. "So, that's how we doing it now. You bad talk me behind my back to your family."

"It wasn't like that. We were all just telling our mother how we felt about her always taking up for ya'll."

"I don't want to hear that shit Gucci. You said all I do is cheat on you. I haven't cheated on you since we made things official. How many times do I have to tell you that?"

"Get your finger out my face. Your past infidelities is the reason why things are the way that they are. If you never would have cheated with Samaya I wouldn't have been getting my assed whooped in front of my daughter. Oh yeah, those hoes totaled my car. I expect a new Benz in my driveway when I wake up in the morning."

"I'm sorry, G. You're right, I fucked up." He pulled me into his embrace and I quickly moved away. I'm not in the mood to be cuddled or patronized.

"You don't have to be sorry but I suggest you be careful. There is no need to get at them bitches on my behalf. I'm handling that myself. I don't want to hear no bullshit excuses about me being your girl and I need to stay home and spend money. Fuck that backseat shit. I'm riding passenger side or driving and I'm still gon' spend money. End of Discussion."

The look on King's face was priceless as I sat on the edge of the bed next to him. I snatched the blunt out of his hand and started smoking.

"Do you want to talk about what just happened between our mothers?"

"Nope."

"You're not the least bit curious about what they were say-ing to each other? I don't know about you but knowing that my father fucked around with your mother has me needing some Lip-ton. That shit was really the tea." On the inside I was embarrassed and wanted to know more about our mothers beef. I couldn't laughing though.

"Why the fuck you laughing, G? Do you think that our mothers were prostitutes and fucking the same nigga is funny? Fuck outta here with that bullshit."

"You're right, baby. I do want to know about that contract Trixie was talking about. I can't wait to call Candy's slick pussy ass."

"Leave that shit alone, Ma. I don't want you opening up a Pandora's box that might hurt you in the end. The last thing I need is my baby in any more pain. I love you, Gucci. Please leave it alone." He kissed me passionately on my lips and I slipped my tongue in his mouth. I would leave it alone for now but I had a funny feeling my nosy ass would eventually open that Pandora's box.

Chapter 18 - Candy

Method to My Madness

Ain't this about a bitch? Out of all the women in the world, the mother of my sons-in-law had to be that hoe Trixie. I went into full attack mode when I saw her. I hated her with a passion. Back in the day, Trixie, our friend Gail, and I all worked for Sincere. The only difference was that I was his bottom bitch. I put in more work for him than those two hoes ever could. I'm the one who gave him three beautiful daughters. It was me who did drug runs with him for Vito Santerelli. We were pulling all types of schemes and scams on the local drug dealers and hustlers from other states. You would think his ass would have been more appreciative. Of course, niggas are never satisfied. Everything was going good until I found out he and Trixie had side shit going on.

I was in shock when I walked in and caught this nigga in my bed with Trixie. Our daughters were in the next room. I just turned and walked out of the room. He would beat my ass if I said a word about what was going on. Sincere was a real asshole. He told me since I didn't know how to knock. Going forward when he had sex with Trixie, I had to join them. I was disgusted. I didn't do pussy but when Sincere gave an order, I followed.

I was so in love him that I was willing to degrade myself just to be with him. The life that we were living was considered lavish back then. I wasn't fucking that up for no bitch, especially not Trixie.

Gail was the smartest out of us. She got as far away from Sincere as she could. Although she was a full-blown dope fiend, she still managed to stop hooking. She met a police officer by the name of Mike Jordan and he did all that he could to get her off the streets. He gave her everything. It didn't matter that she was strung out. I was in shock hearing Trixie reveal that he was King and Nasir's father. I wish I knew where Gail was so I could tell her about that scandalous hoe. It doesn't matter that this shit happened years ago. It's the principle of it all. Her ass has been hiding from the Santerelli Family for all these years. All of a sudden, she pops back up on the scene. Her ass is up to no good. That bitch knows that Gucci, Chanel, and Dior are Sincere's daughters. She might have King and Nasir fooled. I got her number.

No one has seen or heard from her since she went on a drug run with Sincere for Vito Santerelli. They were robbed for over thirty million dollars in cash and drugs. It was story going around that the mob had gunned both of them down.

Sincere's death was hard on me and my girls. I did whatever the fuck I had to do to keep them fed, clothes on their back, and a roof over their head. My daughters mean the world to me. I know that I don't show it but I just don't know how to show it. I guess it's because my mother never hugged me, kissed me, or told me that I was pretty. It's not that I'm not supportive of my girls; I just don't want to baby them when it comes down to the men in their lives. Since the day I met King, Nasir, and Dutch, I knew that they were going to be a force to be reckoned with. I also know for a fact that they love my daughters despite their fuck ups. I see Gucci, Chanel, and Dior being everything I was at their age, Weak and pathetic. Don't no nigga want a weak bitch. The last thing I want is for my girls to become old bitter bitches. Fuck that.

Before it's all said and done Gucci, Chanel, and Dior will reign supreme beside their men and take their rightful places on the throne. When I leave this world, I want them to know how kill to these hoes just by walking in a room and have King, Nasir, and Dutch wrapped around their fingers. Right now, I know that they are pissed off at me and they should be. I need to do better by them. My first step is teaching them the game but first I need to find out what Trixie is up to.

****

It had been two weeks and I hadn't been able to get any information in regard to Trixie. From what I could see, she was in her rehab program and doing everything right. I knew it would be only a matter of time before she slipped up and I would be right there to expose her ass. After calling my daughters for two weeks straight, they finally agreed to come to the house. I decided to cook a big pan of lasagna. I made a salad and garlic bread to go along with it. Once everything was ready and the table was set, the girls arrived.

"I'm so glad ya'll came." I kissed them all on the jaw. Dior and Gucci received me. I could tell Chanel was still a little upset with me. I'm just glad she allowed me to hug and kiss her.

"It smells good in here, Mommy. I'm so hungry," Chanel said as she rubbed her stomach.

"Your ass is always hungry," Gucci said and we all started to laugh.

We walked into the dining room and they sat down. I went and started making their plates. I smiled as I placed their food in front of them. It felt like old times. It had been so long since we all sat down and ate as a family.

"Let me just get to the point why I called you girls over here. I want to start off by saying how sorry I am for everything that I said to you girls. I know you girls think that I don't love you but I do. You are the reason I live and breathe. Everything that I have ever done was to give you a better life. I know my parenting methods have been questionable but I have my reasons. It's not that I take King, Nasir, and Dutch's sides. I know that they love you and they will give you the life I always wanted you girls to have. You don't have to settle for the bullshit that comes along with being with them. However, I need ya'll to stop all that fucking crying and boss the fuck up. They're out there solidifying their spots in the streets. They don't need a weak or pathetic woman at home. What they need is a bitch that will stand beside them and pull the trigger or drive the fucking getaway car. I see you being everything I was and I don't want that for you. I was weak and pathetic for your father up until the day he was killed. When he died, I realized I didn't have shit for our daughters to survive. I knew I had fucked up. There was no way I could have ever been his bottom bitch or the love of his life as he claimed I was. Stop sitting at home just spending money. Get in on the action. Know what's going on with them in the streets. Get a hustle of your own. It doesn't have to be illegal. Just show them that you can bring some shit to the table as well. Let these random bitches know shit ain't sweet. Listen to your momma and everything else will fall into place. I love ya'll with all my heart. All I want is what's best for you. Please forgive me for never showing you the love or affection you deserved."

"We love you too Mommy," my girls all said in unison and got up to hug me. That made me feel better than winning the lottery.

"I'm sorry for the way I spoke to you," Chanel said as she stuffed lasagna in her mouth.

"It's alright, baby. I can't wait for you to give birth to my grandson."

"I can't wait either. He is kicking my butt. I'm tired of pissing on myself if I laugh too hard."

For the rest of the evening we talked. We had so much fun. I could get used to spending quality time with my girls. I was glad they didn't ask about the altercation with Trixie. I wanted to tell them everything once I found out what the bitch was up to.

After they left, I cleaned up and got ready for bed. My doorbell began to ring As soon as I cut all the lights off. I never got visitors besides my kids or my sons-in-law at this time of night. I opened the door without answering and I was in shock at the person standing on the other side of the door. I tried to quickly slam the door but I was met with a bullet between the eyes.

Chapter 19 - King
When It Rains it Pours

I had been out in the streets non-stop since the incident with Gucci and the altercation between our mothers. Samaya had been talking mad shit on Facebook. To add insult injury, someone had uploaded the fight to World Star Hip Hop. That shit had me hot. A part of me wanted to just blow the bitch's brains out but I knew Gucci wanted her get back. So much shit was going on that I couldn't even think straight. I just immersed myself in doing what I had to do to keep the cash flow steady.

It had been a minute since I did a sweep of our traps across the city. Most of the niggas I had working for me never lacked. That's why they were a part of the money team. They knew the rules and were fully aware of the consequences that would come if they fucked up my bread. I cruised down the streets and was impressed at how my young niggas was out grinding and doing their jobs.

Once I was satisfied with the way things were handled, I made my way home to my family. I was glad Gucci had a hairline fracture so they removed the cast and wrapped it up. Her ass had been acting like an invalid. She was working me like a dog around the house. You would have sworn she had on a full body cast.

It was late when I made it to the crib. I already knew Gucci and Imani were asleep. I looked in the microwave and got my dinner plate. I tried to be quiet as possible but Gucci heard me. She could hear a mouse piss on cotton

"What's up, baby. I'm sorry I woke you up," I said as I grabbed a piece of chicken and ate it.

"It's cool. I was waiting up for you anyway. I've been missing you so much."

"You missed daddy, huh? Come and show me how much you

missed me."

Gucci walked towards me seductively and dropped down to her knees. She unbuckled my pants and unleashed the beast. She went straight in for the kill and swallowed my shit whole. I love the fact that she had no gag relax. I could feel my dick down her throat. The sounds of her slurping and moaning were driving a nigga crazy.

"I need to stay gone more often, huh?"

I removed her hair from her face and pulled it up in my hands so that I could see her pretty ass lips glide up and down my shaft. I could feel my nut building up. I applied pressure to the back of her head and pushed her head up and down until I let all my babies loose down her throat. She stood up and bent her over the island. Her pussy was soaking wet so I was able to enter her with the ease. I started off slow. Her shit was feeling so fucking good that I had to go crazy in her. I was trying to murder the pussy.

"God damn, King. Fuck this pussy just like that."

Gucci was screaming out in pleasure and bucking her ass like she was in a rodeo. I was smacking her ass and pulling her at the same time and that only made her ass go crazier. She pushed me back into the chair that I was previously sitting in. She straddled me and began riding me long and hard. Minutes later, both of our asses went crashing to the floor. Gucci was laughing her ass off.

"Oh my God! I can't believe we just broke the fucking chair."

"We ain't do shit. Your ass broke the chair. My whole ass hurts."

We couldn't do shit but laugh. It was times like this that I loved the most about being with Gucci. No matter the situation, she found a way to make me smile. I just stared at her for a minute. I grabbed her face and kissed her lips.

"I love you, Ma.

"I love you too."

Not wanting the moment to end we remained on the kitchen for lost in each other. My cell phone started to ring. I wanted to ignore it but it was Nasir. I was not prepared for the news he delivered. I looked over at my baby and she was still smiling and naked as the day she was born. She and put on her robe and headed upstairs. I had no idea how to tell her Candy had been killed.

I hung up the phone and the sound of her screaming and hollering let me know that she had spoken to one of her sisters. I raced up the stairs to get to her. She was in our bedroom on the floor with her knees pulled up to her chest, rocking bath and forth.

"She was fine when we left. Who could have done this to her?" Gucci laid her head on my shoulder and cried like a baby. I wiped the tears from her eyes with my thumbs and kissed her forehead.

"Don't worry about it. I'm going to find out who did this shit. Let's get dressed so you can meet your sisters at the medical examiner's office."

"Hi Daddy. Is Mommy okay?" Imani stood in the doorway and rubbed her eyes.

"No, baby girl, Mommy is a little sad right now. How about you give her some kisses to make her feel better?" She did as I told her and my phone began to ring. It was Nasir calling again

"What's up Lil Bro?" I asked as I answered the phone.

"Man, get to the hospital quick. Chanel's water broke when she heard about Candy. I'm so nervous right now. I need you, big bro."

"We're on our way. Just get her to the hospital now." I hung up and went back to the bedroom. Gucci was still sitting on the floor and Imani was playing in her hair.

"Chanel's water broke. We need to get to the hospital."

I grabbed her hand and lifted her up from the floor. We both cleaned ourselves up and got dressed. It was really fucking me up in the head that someone violated so close to home. Candy took us in when we didn't have shit. She was like a real mother to us. I needed to understand why someone would want to harm her. Some shit wasn't sitting right. Sooner or later, I was going to get down to the bottom of this shit. For now, my brother needed me beside him. He was about to become a father for the first time and that was the best feeling in the world.

Chapter 20 - Chanel

The Devil is Busy

My water broke as soon as I heard the news. I was cool, calm, and collective but Nasir was so nervous. Nasir was running around the house like a chicken with its head cut off. It was so funny.

"Are you feeling any labor pains yet?" Nasir carried me from the house to the car.

"Just a little pressure in my lower back." I rested my hand on my stomach and exhaled.

"I just want you to know I'm so happy that you're about to give me a son. I love you so much, Ma. I'm sorry about everything. It would mean the world to me if you would give me the honor of being my wife." Nasir was holding the biggest diamond I had ever seen. I couldn't believe he was actually on his knees proposing to me. He knows that I love the color pink. It was a ten-carat princess cut double-tiered engagement ring. It was the most beautiful thing he had ever given me.

"Yessss!" I wrapped my arms around his neck and held onto him for dear life. I didn't want to let him go.

"You just made me the happiest nigga in the world." Nasir grabbed me by the face and tongued me down.

"Ohhh shit!" The pain that shot through my back and my ass had me on the verge of tears.

"Calm down, Ma. We'll be at the hospital shortly."

He grabbed my hand and held on to it. We were almost at the hospital when we came to a red light and had to stop. I looked over at Nasir and he was tapping his fingers against the steering wheel. I reached over and rubbed my fingers through his dreads trying to calm him down. He was so handsome to me. At this very moment there is nowhere else in the world I would rather be than with him. I'm happy he came and got me from Georgia.

For a moment, my mind drifted to my mother. Tears escaped my eyes because of our tumultuous relationship. I just thank God that we were able to make amends before she left this earth.

As I continued to stare at Nasir, a black Expedition pulled alongside of us. I didn't have time to react before I saw the window come down and a gun pointed at him. The last thing I remembered was the sound of gunfire and bullets hitting the car. Nasir never got a chance to return fire. He jumped on top of me to shield my body. The gunfire seemed to go on forever. Suddenly it stopped and a wave of pain shot through my entire body. Nasir was on top of me and wasn't moving at all.

"Nasir! Baby wake up. Please wake up." I could hear him gurgling as he tried to speak but no words were actually coming out. I began to scream and panic.

"Please somebody help me!" All of sudden the doors were pulled open by King, Dutch and some of their men. I could hear Gucci and Dior crying as well.

"Help him ya'll! I don't think he's breathing!"

"Don't do this shit to me, lil bro." I watched as King kicked the car repeatedly. Nasir's body was moved from our car into another car. Dutch picked me up and carried me to the car my sisters were in. My labor pains had kicked in full speed ahead.

"Take her to the hospital right now!" Dutch was covered in blood and I lost my cool. Gucci immediately drove off.

"Oh my God! He's dead, isn't he?" I lost my cool and I started to hyperventilate.

"No he's not. Just calm down, Chanel. We'll be at the hospital in a minute."

Dior was trying her best to calm me down but I started going crazy; kicking the seats and banging on the windows. I was acting a damn fool. The doctors were in the Emergency entrance working on Nasir when we made it. I was fighting my sisters and the doctors. I saw one of the doctor's with a big ass needle getting ready to stick me. I tried my best to fight his ass. I was no match for whatever was in that needle. As soon as he stuck me in the arm, I became numb. I didn't drift into unconsciousness immediately. My eyes were fixated on the doctor pounding up and down on Nasir's chest. He was just lying there bloody and lifeless. I closed my eyes and prayed to God that he would be okay.

****

The sound of Dior and Gucci's voice brought me out of my slumber. I looked around and tried to remember where I was. I looked over and Gucci was holding a baby. My hand immediately went to my stomach. There was still a bulge but it was no longer big as it was. I started to stir around in the bed.

"I'm so happy you're awake, Chanel. Here is your son. Nasir Jr. is just perfect. He looks just like his daddy." Gucci and Dior were crying as they handed me my son. As I looked at him, all I could see were the bloody images of his father.

"Where is Nasir?" I whispered. Gucci and Dior just stood there looking at me with sad eyes.

"He's on life support. They don't think he will ever wake up. King wanted to wait until you woke up to see what you wanted to do."

"What the fuck you mean what I wanted to do? I want him to remain on life support. He is not going to do die. He has to be here to raise his son and plan our wedding. Tell the nurse to come get the baby. I want to see him. He needs to hear my voice."

There so much hitting me at once. I laid my head back and cried river of tears. The Devil is working overtime on my family and I don't know why.

After the nurse got the baby, they wheeled me upstairs to the trauma unit. King, Dutch, and Thug were already in his room when I got in there. They all looked at me with sad eyes.

King knelt in front of me and held my hands inside of his. "I already know they told you about his condition. I really don't want him to suffer but whatever you decide is what we'll roll with."

"I'm not pulling the plug on him. Let me take him home. He needs to be at home with his family." King nodded in agreement and everyone left the room.

"Make sure you let me or Tahari know if you need anything."

Thug kissed me on my jaw and left the room. I could tell he was hurt. He loved Nasir like blood. I pushed my wheelchair over to his bed and all I could do was cry. He had tubes coming from everywhere. I managed to stand up and place kisses all over his face.

"Nasir, you have to wake up. Our son needs to meet his daddy. Plus, I have so many ideas for our wedding. I'm not giving up on you. I'm taking you home and nurse you back to health. You can't leave me here all alone to raise our baby. I need you now more than ever. Please come back to me. I love you so much, baby." I gave him one last kiss and I left the room. I wanted to be with my son. He needed me.

Chapter 21 - Dior

Don't Fuck With My Heart

The next couple of weeks were a complete blur. My mother's death and Nasir basically being kept alive was a lot on all of us, Especially King and Dutch. They had been basically living in the streets killing any and every fucking body they thought had something to do with the shit. My mother didn't want a funeral. For as long as I could remember, she always said that she wanted to be cremated. She said she didn't want any phony bitches at her funeral acting like they loved or liked her. We respected her wishes and cremated her. We each got a portion of her ashes.

With everything that had been going on, Dutch was never at home. I was lonelier than ever. Both of my sisters had children and that took up all of their time. A part of me knew I was being self-centered. I hated to see Chanel going through this. She insisted on taking care of her newborn baby and Nasir. It just kind of bothered me knowing both of my sisters were mothers. I put on a brave face in front of them and Dutch but on the inside, I was kind of jealous.

Dutch bought me a new house. It was beautiful and spacious. Recently, I ran into this guy named Lucky that I used to go to school with. We had met up for dinner a couple of times. Just friendly conversation nothing more. A part of me knew that I was wrong. I was going out on dates with another man. I just loved Lucky's conversation. He was so gentle. Dutch was rough and we barely held a conversation.

Tonight, I was meeting Lucky at Chili's for drinks. I knew that Dutch would be out all night because it was the first of the month. I put on a cute little sweater dress with some thigh high riding boots. I made it to the restaurant a little late. Lucky was already there waiting on me.

"I thought you weren't going to make it." Lucky got up and pulled my chair out for me. He was looking good as usual.

"I'm sorry. I took nap and I overslept.

"Hey, I'm your waitress, Natavia. Are you guys ready to order?"

I took in her appearance. She was a nice looking plus-sized chick. She had long Senegalese twists. I could tell she thought she was the shit the way she cheesing all hard at Lucky. These bitches don't even care about flirting with another nigga in front of the female that they are with. I'm not in a relationship with him but damn bitch have some respect.

"Yes. I'll have the spinach dip, the steak quesadillas, and a pomegranate margarita," I said as I rolled my eyes and handed her the menu.

"Anything for you, sir?"

"Yes. I'll have the loaded potato skins, half of slab of ribs, and a Heineken."

The waitress took our menus. The bitch was really pissing me off with the sly grin she had on her face. I shook the shit off and continued on with dinner with Lucky. I enjoyed myself. It felt like I hadn't laughed in so long. I found myself staring at him from time to time. His smile was intoxicating. He was full of life. Lately Dutch was damn down in the dumps.

"We have got to do this again," Lucky said as he walked me to my car.

"Yes. I had so much fun with you."

He leaned in and kissed me on the lips. I quickly moved away from him. I was shocked that he had done that.

"I'm sorry. I shouldn't have done that."

"It's okay. I need to get going. I'll give you a call tomorrow."

I gave him a quick hug and jumped inside my car. I took a deep breath as I pulled away. I couldn't go out with him anymore. I didn't like the way the kiss made me feel. It was almost three in the morning when I got home. I got straight in the shower. I smelled like Jean Paul Gaultier. I had to hurry up and get in the shower and wash his scent off of me. The shower curtain being jerked back caused me to jump.

"Oh shit. You scared the fuck out of me, Dutch." I held my hand over my chest trying to catch my breath. I looked at Dutch and he had a mean mug on his face. Fear instantly set in. I had seen him look like that before. I knew nothing good would come from it.

"Get the fuck out of the shower!"

"Why? What's wrong with you?"

"I said get the fuck out of the shower."

Dutch was dragging me out of the shower by my hair. I could feel my hair being ripped from my scalp. He threw me on the floor in our bedroom. Dutch was standing over me

"I never knew you were a sneaky conniving ass bitch."

"Please, Dutch, tell me what's going on. What are you talking about?"

"Who the fuck were you out with tonight?" His fists were balled up and his jaws were clenched. I knew he was about to whoop my ass. I just sat there too scared to speak. Tears rolled down my face and that's when I felt the first slap to my face.

"Your ass is out cheating with some lame, bitch ass nigga. You giving that nigga my pussy?"

He was now stomping and kicking me repeatedly. I was trying my best to ball up to keep him from breaking my ribs. Those damn Timberlands hurt like a bitch.

"I'm not cheating on you. I swear to God. I love you. Please don't hit me anymore."

He yanked me up from the floor and threw me on the bed. Dutch was standing at the foot of the bed unbuckling his belt. I hoped and prayed he wasn't about to beat me with it.

"See this picture I have in my phone tells me differently."

He climbed on top of me and started choking me with all his might. At the same time, he was showing me the picture of Lucky kissing me on the lips and of me hugging him good-bye. It looked all bad on my end. All I could do was cry.

"Please let me explain. It's not what you think."

"Ain't shit to explain. It's not what I think. It's a matter of what the fuck I see with my own eyes. Since you want to act like hoe.

That's how I'm going to treat you. Dutch was now prying my legs a part roughly at the same time trying to ram his dick inside of me. I couldn't believe he was doing this to me at this moment.

"Please Dominique, don't do this."

"Shut the fuck up." The punch he delivered to my mouth made me do as he said. I just laid there and cried as he roughly fucked me. It felt like he was ripping me with each thrust. He raped for about ten minutes before he came long and hard. For a minute, he laid on top of me breathing hard like a wild animal. I wasn't even crying anymore. I just laid there in a daze.

"Now get the fuck out bitch. I'm done with your tramp ass."

He walked out of the room and I heard the front door slam. At that moment, I regretted going out with Lucky. If the shoe was on the other foot, I know that I would be mad too. I didn't know if I mad at him for doing this to me or mad because I got caught. I managed to crawl out of bed and clean myself up. My face was bruised and swollen. My lip was split as well. My legs and my pussy were aching. I cried as I sat inside the hot water in the bath-tub. When I was finished, it was too late at night for me to leave. I put on a pair of jeggings and a t-shirt and lay across the bed in the guest bedroom. I would leave first thing in the morning.

Hours later, the sound of the headboard banging up against the wall and moaning woke me up from my sleep. At first, I thought I was dreaming, but the sound of a bitch screaming Dutch's name made me know this was no fucking dream. I got up and walked towards our room. The door was already open. My chest began to hurt as I observed them having wild passionate sex. Tears streamed from my eyes as they switched positions. She looked up and we locked eyes. It was the waitress from Chili's. Now all the shit started to make since. This hoe had set me up to get caught by Dutch.

"You sneaky bitch!" I dived on top them. I was beating the shit out of her .I didn't care that she was naked. She was trying her best use her weight against me but I overpowered her ass. I dragged that bitch out the bed and got on top of her and started raining blows down on that ass. I completely blacked out. All I could see was Dutch whooping my ass. I was mad at him for killing our baby. I was mad at God for taking away my mother. Her ass was feeling the pain of everything that I had been through.

"Get this crazy bitch off of me, Dutch!" she screamed as I started to bang her head into the floor. Before I knew it, Dutch was picking me up and carrying me out of the room.

"Don't bring your ass out of this room, Natavia!" he said to her as he closed the room door behind him.

"Let me the fuck go! How could you bring another bitch in my house? That bitch is the one that sent you those pictures of me. Nigga, your black ass ain't slick. You've been cheating on me with her all along. You're a grimy motherfucker!"

I charged his ass and started fucking him up. We were knocking all the pictures off the wall along the hallway. This nigga thought he was about to dog me without it being a motherfucking fight. He was naked as the day he was born. I went for his dick but he slapped me hard as hell. I lost my balance and fell. He pinned me down to the floor and put his knee in my throat.

"Get the fuck out of here with that bullshit, Dior. Your hoe ass started this shit and I'm going to finish it. If you don't want your feelings hurt or your ass beat, I suggest you leave. In case you didn't hear me earlier, I'm done with your ass."

Those words hurt my heart, my soul, and my spirit. I swallowed the huge lump in my throat. I wanted to cry but I knew that it wouldn't change the way Dutch felt about me. He still had his knee pressed down in my throat. I could barely breathe. I just wanted him to remove his knee.

"I'm going to let you up but if you swing on me, I'm going to beat your ass."

I knew that Dutch was trying to hear shit I was saying. However, I felt the need to explain. I slowly got off the floor and was prepared to leave. Knowing that another bitch was lying in my bed, in my new house let me know he was done with me. I knew this bitch was after his bread. He would find that shit out in the end. I couldn't wait to catch that bitch in traffic. Every time I saw her, I was tagging that ass.

"I know you don't believe me and I don't expect you too. I just want you to know that I never had sex with Lucky. Goodbye, Dominique."

I turned and walked away from him. I didn't even bother to grab any of my belongings. I left with the clothes I had on my back and my purse. I got in my car and got ready to drive off but something clicked in my head. I grabbed my Kush blunt from the ashtray and flamed it up. I took a couple of puffs and put it out. I hopped out and went around back to the tool shed. I found a big can of gasoline. I couldn't believe what I was about to do. I had to send Dutch a message loud and clear. He might have thought I was a weak bitch but she died when I caught him with Natavia. Her fucking name made my ears hurt. He said her name with so much passion when he told her to stay in the room. I'm going beat her for that too.

Both of their cars were parked in the driveway. I started dousing both of their cars with the gasoline. I used my house keys to go in the front door. I knew they were probably upstairs fucking. I laughed as I poured gasoline all over the living room and dining room area. I made sure to pour gasoline in the coat closet. I wanted to burn all his Pelle Pelle coats, Retro Jordans, and his minks. I could imagine his face if he made it out the fire to know he didn't have some of his most prized possessions. I held the lighter up against one of the coats and everything immediately was engulfed in flames.

I ran out of the front door and did the same thing to his Range and her Impala. I hopped back in my car and turned my radio on sky high. Ironically, *Let It Burn* by Usher was playing on the radio. I laughed my ass off as I peeled out of the driveway. I looked in the rearview mirror and all I saw was flames in the distance. I hoped and prayed I burned him and that bitch alive. It would serve him right. Dutch had been cheating on me all the time with that bitch. This would teach his ass not to play with my heart.

Chapter 22 - Gucci

Never Saw It Coming

Lately King had been going through so much. Nasir being in the state that he was in it had my baby fucked up. King felt like he failed Nasir. When Trixie walked out on them, King made it his sole responsibility to take care of his little brother. King was fucked up behind what happened to Nasir. The machines were keeping Nasir alive. He would be dead without them. Chanel wasn't accepting that. She held on to the hope that he would come out of this but all of us knew that Nasir would never wake up. King wanted to take him off the machines but out of respect for Chanel, he let her make all of the decisions. King hasn't been to see Nasir since Chanel too him home. He couldn't bear to look at him like that. Instead, he had lost himself in the bottle. The streets were feeling my baby's wrath. He was sparing no one's life until he found who did this shit to Nasir.

I'm so worried about Chanel. She's so overwhelmed but refuses to let anyone help. Despite that, I've been doing a little dirt. I've been keeping tabs on this Samaya

Tonight was the night I was getting this bitch back for jumping on me. I could never catch her by herself until tonight. I had been sitting outside her house on the far south side of Chicago in the Wild Hundreds. No one had come in or left. I sat in my rental and watched her every move. She emerged slowly from her burnt orange Charger and went inside her house.

I sat in the car with my gun in my hand. Since the incident at the mall, I had been going to the gun range with Tahari and her sister Keesha every week. They were both so down to Earth. I loved kicking it with them. They had been schooling me on so much shit. Keesha was nutty as hell. I thought Tahari was crazy but Keesha was a damn nutcase.

When King found out we had been hanging out, all he could do was shake his head. The last thing he wanted was Tahari grooming me into her protégé. I needed to focus on something other than all the sad shit that was plaguing my family.

I hadn't smoked a cigarette in years. King hated for me to smoking cigarettes. He said it was unladylike. Since I was his lady, I should never ever think of smoking. However, I needed a Newport bad as hell to calm my nerves. I was getting ready to get out but a car pulled up. I was speechless as King got out and jogged up her front stairs. I was mad as hell because I had told him to let me handle this shit. I watched as he went inside her house with a key. There was nothing I could do because I had lied and told him that I was going to help Chanel out.

I was getting ready to just drive away but something inside of me was saying follow through with my original plan. King would have to just deal with it. I exited my car and tucked my gun in the small of my back. I exhaled and walked up to the front door. From the other side I could hear him and her in a heated argument.

At first, I wanted to stand there and listen to the door but there was nothing for them to talk about. He was supposed to blow that bitch brains out and keep it the fuck moving. I decided to knock on the door and let my presence be known. I banged on the door relentlessly until someone answered.

"Who the fuck is it?" Samaya said as she flung the door open.

"Your worst nightmare, bitch!"

I hit that bitch across her the nose with the butt of my gun. I heard it crack on impact. I started pistol-whipping her. She started to fight back and we both ended up falling and fighting on the floor. We started to tussle over the gun and it went off. I didn't feel any pain so I knew she was the one that was hit. I pushed her off of me and she was hit in the chest. She was still alive but not for long. Blood was pouring from her mouth.

"What the fuck did you do?"

"It's that bitch's fault. She never should have tried to jump bad. She should have taken that ass whooping like a woman. Let me find out you concerned about this bitch."

"I'm not thinking about her ass. This is messy. You know I don't move like this and you know it. I need to clean this shit up. Go home right now!"

"I can't believe you right now, King."

"Shut the fuck up, Gucci, and go home. Don't make me tell your ass again."

He started walking towards me and I got the fuck out of dodge. I headed straight to my house. I couldn't wait until King brought his ass home. We were about to straight have it out. I was glad Imani was at a slumber party at Barbie's house. We just might come to blows.

As I walked up to my door, I never saw the person behind me until I was being dragged off the porch and a rag was being placed over my mouth. I kicked and screamed until my body went limp and I slipped into unconsciousness.

Chapter 23 - King

Secret No More

Knowing that Nasir was never waking up took a toll on me. He was all I had in this world besides Gucci and Imani. Life without him wouldn't even be worth living. I couldn't stand to see him just lying there looking like he was dead. That shit started to spook me out so I stopped going to see him altogether. I had been finding solace in a bottle of Remy and Kush blunt after Kush blunt. All I wanted to do was numb the pain that I felt in my heart.

Despite feeling down, I still did what the fuck I had to do as far as my business was concerned. I had got word that Samaya's older brother, Vino, was behind Nasir getting gunned down. Recently Nasir had kicked his ass off of the Money Team due to him coming up short with his count more than once. I should have cut his ass off when I cut his sister's off. Word was those bitches were in on the hit too. Not to mention they would probably be gunning for me next. I like to move in silence and logically. I'm not into that wild gun toting shit. I already had my plan into motion. I had Samaya thinking that we could start fucking around again and that I was going to put her back on the team. Of course her dick silly ass couldn't wait to wrap her lips around my shit. I knew it was time for me to get rid of her ass. That time came sooner than I expected when she called and said she had to talk to me about something. I immediately went to her house.

As soon as I walked in, I slapped fire from her ass. That's when we started to argue. I was getting ready to get some information out of her about her involvement in Nasir's shooting but Gucci brought her ass there and killed the damn girl. I was getting ready to torch the house when I heard someone come through the front door. Thank God that I had already moved Samaya to the basement.

"Maya, where are you?" her sister Samina called.

Shit had just get better for me especially since that bitch was involved as well. I was caught off guard when I heard what sounded like a child's voice saying "Mommy." I came from the back and let my presence be known. The bitch looked like she had seen a ghost. She knew what was up.

"Please, King, don't kill me!"

I watched as she pushed the little boy behind her. I was able to get a good look at him before she did and he looked just like Imani. He looked to be about six years old. Around the time when I hooked up with Gucci. I would sleep with Samaya from time to time. She came to me one day talking about she was pregnant. Of course I gave the bitch money for an abortion. I even dropped her off and picked her up after the procedure. I never told anyone about her being pregnant.

"Daddy! Please don't hurt my, TeTe."

I hid my gun behind my back and gestured for him to come to me. "I'm not your father, lil man. Who told you that?"

"My mommy showed me pictures of you on her Facebook page and said that you were my daddy. She said that I have a little sister named Imani. Are you here to come and get me like she promised?"

All the air had left my body. She had lied all this years. I wish I could bring the bitch back to life and kill her ass all over again. I looked at Samina and the look on her face confirmed my biggest fear.

"What's your name, lil man?"

"King Carter Jr. but everybody calls me KJ."

He was every bit of me as he spoke with such confidence. I whispered in his ear and told him to go pack a him some clothes. He came back from his room carrying a book bag. I told him to wait for me in my car. I made sure to describe it to him so that he would know which one it was. When I was sure he was inside, I focused on Samina.

"Before you say anything King. I didn't have nothing-."

I silenced her ass with a bullet right between the eyes. Two snake in the grass bitches down. I dragged her body down the stairs and doused both of them with gasoline then lit their asses on fire. I went upstairs and poured gasoline all over everything upstairs and did the same. I lit the match and got out of there with the quickness.

For a brief moment, I forgot all about the little boy in the back seat until he spoke up.

"I'm so happy you came and rescued me."

"What do you mean rescued you?"

"My mommy used to lock me in the closet if I cried. She used to whoop me with a coat hanger. She said I looked just like your no good ass."

This shit had me all fucked up in the head. I hated for any child to be mistreated. I looked at him through the rearview mirror and knew he was mine. I was going to do everything in my power to give him the life he deserved to have. My only concern was Gucci and how she was going to deal with me having a son. Most likely, she wouldn't accept it. I really don't expect her too. Right now, he needs me and I'm not turning my back on him for nobody, not even for the love of my life.

When I pulled into my driveway, I let out a deep breath because I knew Gucci was about to go crazy. When I made to the door, I knew something was terribly wrong. Her keys were still inside the door and one of her shoes was on the doorstep. It was obvious that someone had taken her.

"No! No! No!" I said as I tapped my gun up against my temple.

KJ was looking like he was scared so I put the gun away. I couldn't believe a motherfucker had violated my wife and my home. No one even knew where we laid our heads so this shit was close to home. I had to take KJ somewhere safe and the only person I could think of was Chanel. I called the rehab as I made my way over to Chanel's house. I was informed that Trixie was no longer at the treatment center. I knew that bitch couldn't kick the habit. I thought that she would at least come and check on Nasir but she never came. I had officially washed my hands of her crack head ass. My mind was going into overdrive trying to figure out who the fuck had my girl. I called an emergency meeting and I wanted all hands on deck.

I pulled into Chanel's driveway and realized shit wasn't right over here either. The damn door was wide open. Not to mention Dior's car was in the driveway

"Stay in here, KJ, until I come back."

"Okay Daddy."

He calling me Daddy was growing on me already. He was the only bright spot I had right now. I walked up to the door and I could hear Lil Nasir screaming at the top of his lungs. I walked slowly through the house with my gun down to my side. I headed straight to the nursery. Lil Nasir was in his crib crying his heart out. He was soaking wet and cold because he had no clothes on, not even a pamper. I looked around and I noticed Chanel must have just given the baby a bath. She had his little clothes laid out that she was going to dress him in.

"Shhh! Come on phew-phew. Uncle King got you. It's okay, lil man." I rocked him back and forth until he stopped crying. He was sucking all on his fingers. I knew that meant he was hungry. I went in search of his formula.

"Daddy, you straight?"

"I thought I told you to stay in the car."

"I know you did but you were gone for too long so I started to get worried."

This little nigga was gone be something else. He had an old soul to only be six. I warmed the baby up a bottle and put him on some dry clothes. Not long after he ate, he was fast asleep. I held on to him and then all of sudden it cliqued in my head that Nasir was in the back room. I went to the back where he was. KJ was hot on my heels. I couldn't believe it Nasir was laying there with his eyes wide open. He was unable to move because he had restraints and unable to speak because he had tubes down his throat. He just kept blinking. I guess he saw me holding the baby and knew he was his son.

"He's cool, lil bro."

I laid him on his chest and he started to shed tears. I called our private doctor and told him to come quick. I also called the crew and told them to come here for the meetings. Chanel, Dior, and Gucci were missing and I had a pretty good idea of who had them.

Chapter 24 - Dutch

Hot Nigga

As soon as Dior left out of the house, I went inside the bedroom to check on Natavia. She was lying in bed waiting for me.

"You straight, Ma?"

"Hell no. That bitch tried to kill me. She better be lucky I'm pregnant or I would have beat her ass."

I have been fucking with Natavia for a couple of months. We were more off than on because I was trying to do right by Dior. Plus, Natavia was becoming so clingy since she found out that she was pregnant, Three months to be exact. I knew I had to do the right thing by her when I found out she was carrying my seed. It was as if God was giving me a second chance at being a father. The incident between me and Dior had put a big strain on our relationship. Dior wasn't fucking with me so I went to the one person I knew that would. Natavia had been comfort and a peace of mind helping me deal with the loss of the baby that Dior was carrying.

I felt like shit when I was fucking with Natavia because Dior was a good girl. That was until Natavia called me and told me to come up to Chili's because she had something I might want to see.

Lucky always had a thing for Dior. She swore up and down she wasn't checking for him. He was mad because King would no longer front him dope. I wanted to put a bullet in both of their fucking heads.

"What are you over there thinking about?" Natavia asked. She crawled to edge of the bed and started massaging my dick.

I let out a slight moan as she placed it in her mouth and started giving me that sloppy toppy. Her head game was A-1 but she was no Dior. My dick went limp as the sadness in Dior's face appeared in my head. I knew her seeing me fucking another woman had hurt her. I never would have even brought Natavia to the crib if I had known she was still there. A part of me was trying to be comfortable with the situation because now she felt my pain. The other part of me was fucked up because I had already caused her so much pain. This was icing on the cake I knew that we were officially over. All the trust was gone on both of our parts.

"What the fuck is that smell?" I sniffed in the air and it smelled like some shit was on fire. I pushed Natavia off of me and put on my boxers. Instantaneously, fire alarms were going off. I looked out the window and my truck was up in flames. So was Natavia's car.

"Put on some clothes." Natavia jumped up and started to put on clothes. As soon as I opened the bedroom door, I saw nothing but smoke. The flames from the downstairs were starting to rise.

"Oh my God! How are we going to get out of here?" Natavia was now crying and panicking.

"We need to climb out the window. That's the only way out."

"I hope you know her crazy ass set the house on fire. Not to mention my fucking car. You need to do something about her psychotic ass. I'm pressing charges against that bitch."

"Shut the fuck up. Your ass ain't pressing shit. I'll handle Dior."

The smoke was starting to get thicker and we both were starting to choke. I managed to throw on a pair of basketball shorts and grab my phone. By the time we were climbing out of the window, a fire truck was pulling up and my nosy ass neighbors were out on their lawns. I couldn't believe Dior had done this shit. I was going beat her ass for burning down a brand new fucking house. I was glad that I hadn't moved my guns or my safes out of the old crib just yet.

"Is everyone out of the house?" a fireman asked us.

We both nodded yeah. Not long after the fire was put out and the fire marshal was accessing the situation. I had been trying to get in contact with King and Dior but both of their phones were going straight to voicemail.

"One of my men found a gas can on the lawn. This was arson. Do you have any idea who would want to burn your house down?"

"No sir, I don't have a clue."

"Bullshit, Dutch! His girlfriend, Dior Lennox, did this shit and I want to press charges. I'm three months pregnant and she assaulted me. Not to mention she tried to kill us by setting the house on fire."

Natavia was singing like a bird and that sealed whatever future we could have. The bitch was a fucking snitch. I told her ass not to do that. I wanted to choke the shit out of her. She was giving a statement to the police. Rat ass bitch. I heard them putting out an APB out on Dior's car. As soon as they left, I popped her ass in the mouth.

"Why the fuck did you hit me?" She was holding her mouth and blood was seeping out between her fingers.

"You already know why I hit your stupid ass. I told your ass not to press charges. I'm done fucking with your rat ass. Get home the best way that you can. I'll buy you a new car. After that, we're finished. Don't call me until you give birth to my seed."

"She tried to kill us and you're taking her side. I knew you still loved that hoe. You think I'm about to let you do me dirty. Nigga, I'm the queen of doing a motherfucker dirty. Fuck you and fuck this baby too. Call me what you want. I'll be in court when they catch the bitch."

Natavia starting walking off and I was about to break my foot off in her ass for her mouth. My phone started ringing. It was King. I had to sit down on the curb and take in everything that he was saying to me.

At that moment, I didn't give a fuck about Dior being with that nigga or her burning up my car or our house. I definitely didn't give a fuck about Natavia anymore. She had me fucked all the way up. Dior was still my baby and someone had violated me in the worst possible way. All bets were off when I found out who the fuck had my girl and her sisters.

Chapter 25 - Gucci
Wolves in Sheep's Clothing

I had been trying to untie myself for hours with no such luck. I needed to help Chanel and Dior. They were both lying on the floor beside me unconscious but they weren't tied up. I guess whoever took us had knocked them out with the same shit that was used on me. I had no idea who kidnapped us or why. I looked around and tried to figure out where we were being held. We were in a basement. I looked over and saw that Dior was starting to wake up. She sat up and started rubbing her head.

"My head is hurting like a motherfucker."

"Untie me, Dior."

She looked over and managed to make it over to me. Chanel was starting to wake up too.

"What the hell is going on?" Chanel said as she sat all the way up.

"We've been kidnapped. That's what the hell is going on. Let's try to get the out of here," I said as Dior was finally able to untie me. We got up and started banging on windows and trying to get out of the door. We had no such luck.

"I wonder if someone made it to my house yet. Nasir needs his injections and all I could remember was my baby crying at the top of his lungs. Please Lord, let my babies be okay."

"They're okay. Calm down. We need to be focused and figure who the fuck has us. Plus, you already know King and Dutch are out handling shit."

I had all the confidence in the world when it came down to King. Whoever did this better get right with God because King was coming with guns blazing.

"Hopefully, Dutch made it out of the fire," Dior said with tear streaming down her face.

"What fire?" Chanel and I said at the same time.

"I set the house on fire with Dutch and his bitch inside. The whole thing was engulfed in flames. How could he bring her to my house he had just bought me?"

We huddled close and tried to console each other. I felt sorry for Dior because she and Dutch just couldn't get it together. It had to be hard on her to see our relationships changing for the better.

"Well, I see the sleeping beauties are now awake," a female's voice said as she walked in the door.

She was dressed in a black leather jumpsuit and thigh high boots. I couldn't believe who it was. She looked different but I knew it was still her. She was carrying a big ass shot gun.

"Why are you doing this to us, Trixie?"

"Why are you doing this to us, Trixie?" She mocked Chanel. "Shut the fuck up. You remind me of your dead ass mother with all that whining and shit. I don't see how King or Nasir deal with you spoiled whiney ass bitches."

"Bitch, you're just jealous because they love us and hate your crack head ass. My mother was right about you. You're a low down dirty bitch. We are the mothers of your grandchildren. What about them?"

"What about them little fuckers? In case you forgot I don't care about my own kids. Why would I give a fuck about their kids? Fuck all of this mushy shit. Get that nigga King on the phone." Not long after a man came into the room.

"You're in on this shit too, Lucky." Dior was now standing to her feet trying to rush him but he hit her so hard upside her head with the butt of his gun that she dropped instantly.

"Shut the fuck up! You should have given me some pussy. I might have spared your ass. I'm running this show here."

He pulled a chair up and sat directly in front of us. "Dial that niggas number right now. I'm sick of looking at you bitches." Trixie shoved the phone in my hand and I dialed King's number. He answered on the second ring. I put it on speakerphone.

"Baby, it's me."

"Are you okay? Are Chanel and Dior with you?"

"Yeah, they're here."

Lucky snatched the phone from my hand. "King, my nigga! What it do? I got your bitch and her two sisters. I have enough dick to give these bitches all night."

"Nigga, you better not lay a finger on them. Who the fuck is this and what the fuck do you want?"

"My feelings are hurt. It's ya boy, Lucky. How is Nasir? I heard my shot was a little off. I won't miss next time." Lucky let out an evil laugh that sent Chanel over the edge. She pounced on Lucky. They were rolling around on the floor tussling over the gun

"Gucci! Gucci!" King was calling me through the phone but I couldn't answer. I had to help my sisters.

Trixie and Dior were tussling as well. The shotgun flew out of her hands and I grabbed it. I swung around and blew Lucky's chest open. He fell off of Chanel. I turned around to shoot that bitch but she was gone. Dior was looking woozy. Chanel and I ran over to help her.

"Come on, Dior, we have to go before the police come."

We went over to the door where Trixie had escaped. We were being held in someone's home. Once we made it outside, I looked around. We were around a lot of vacant buildings by some railroad tracks. I didn't even realize I still had the phone in my hand. It started ringing so I answered it. It was King.

I described our surroundings. Within a matter of minutes, some of his men were pulling up and I was so happy. I was confused as to why they kidnapped us. Why in the hell would Trixie want to hurt her own kids? I knew shit was about to get real when we were being escorted to Thug's massive estate. Once we entered the gate, we headed straight to the guesthouse. King and Dutch were standing outside.

"I'm not getting out this car. He is not about to beat my ass," Dior said as she folded her hands across her chest. King yanked the door open and I jumped out in his arms.

"Did that motherfucker put his hands on you?" I shook my head as King looked me over for signs that I was hurt.

"Where is my baby?"

"He's in the house with Nasir. He woke up last night." Chanel took off running and screaming into the house. Dior was still in the car refusing to get out.

"Get the fuck out of the car before I yank your ass out." Dutch squeezed the bridge of his nose trying to calm down. "I don't want to fight with you, Dior. I'm glad you're okay. I was worried sick about you. Please get out of the car and come inside. Your head is bleeding."

Dior finally stepped out of the car and followed Dutch inside. I was glad because I was in no mood to kick his ass today.

"Baby, before we go inside, I need to holler at you real quick," King said as he wrapped his arms around my waist.

"Are you going to finish playing NBA 2K14 with me, Daddy?"

We both turned around and I looked a little boy who was the splitting image of my daughter. I started shaking uncontrollably. My tears were blinding me. Dior, Dutch, and Chanel were standing in the doorway. I felt like I was going to pass out.

"I was only kidnapped for one day. I come back and you have a son. Who's his mother?" I was looking directly into King's eyes. Tears were streaming down my face.

"Samaya is his mother. I-"

King was still talking but I went deaf after hearing the name he said. I don't know what came over me. I just took off running like I was Forrest Gump. I could hear King behind me but I was too fast. As soon as I made it in front of the main house Tahari was getting out of her car and walking up to her door. I ran inside behind her and locked the door.

"Please don't let King in."

"Why are you running from him?"

"What the fuck is all this noise down here?" Thug walked straight to the door and opened it. King rushed in, yanked me by my arm, and tried to pull me out of the door.

"I'm not finished talking to you."

"Let me go. Just leave me alone." I was trying my best to get away from him.

"Thug, you go talk to King. I'll try to calm Gucci down." Tahari grabbed me and pulled me towards her.

"I hate your ass!" I said to King as I spit on him. Before I knew it, King was beating my ass. It took Thug and Tahari a minute to get his ass off of me.

"Bitch, don't you ever do no nasty shit like that again."

He shook the shit out of me and then threw my ass on the floor. He walked out the door and Thug went after him.

"Damn, G, Why would you spit on him?" Tahari said as she helped me up off the floor.

"He has a son on me with that bitch Samaya. How could he do this to me?" I cried like a baby on Tahari's shoulder. My lip and my nose were bleeding. Tahari took me upstairs and cleaned me up. I was in shock at all the events that had taken place in the last twenty-four hours. All I wanted to do was wake up from this nightmare called my life. I just keep hearing that little boy call him Daddy. Tears streamed down my face. My heart and soul was aching. I cried until I drifted off to sleep.

Chapter 26 - Tahari

Devious Intentions

I felt really bad for Gucci. she had been through so much shit lately. I know what it's like to constantly be hit with bullshit. If it ain't one thing it's another when you fucking with a Thug Inc nigga. They love the shit out of us but they stay doing bullshit that has the potential to lose us.

Gucci had heart to spit on King though. Thug would have knocked all my fucking teeth down my throat. Despite not being the type of man that doesn't hit women. That would be the ultimate disrespect. I tried talking to Gucci but she was too upset to cry. I just gave her some privacy and time to get herself together. Whether she wanted to or not eventually she would have to sit down and talk with King. The only reason King wasn't dragging her ass out of here now. Is because Thug told him to fallback. They were having a meeting in the conference room and from the sounds off all the commotion. They wouldn't be coming out anytime soon. I couldn't believe King and Nasir's mother had something to do with kidnapping them damn girls .Then again after what my parents did to me there is nothing that surprises me anymore.

I knew that everybody would be hungry once the meeting was over so I ordered some pans of chicken and Fish. I prepared spaghetti and a Garden Salad as the side dishes.

I thumbed through the mail as I waited for the cheese to melt on top of the spaghetti. A certified letter from my doctor was amongst the pile. I immediately opened it up. I had been waiting for my test results. I had been feeling under the weather lately. I had an inkling that I had Cancer or something. As I read the letter I almost passed out. I know damn well this letter wasn't saying that I was pregnant. I know for a fact I got my tubes tied. So, either this was a mix-up or somebody about to get the shit sued out of them. I had a copy of all my medical records from when I gave birth in Miami. I remember signing paperwork as consent to get my tubes tied. I found the file in my office and thumbed through it. There was no paper in there with me giving consent to get my tubes tied. I found the doctor's number that delivered Kaia and Kahari. I was glad that when I called, he picked up. I flat out asked him did he tie my tubes. Instead, the motherfucker told me no and he was following orders from Mr. Kenneth. I knew then Thug paid him not to tie my tubes. I just hung up the phone and sat on the bar stool. Why would Ka'Jaire do this to me? He knew how I felt about already having seven damn kids. I know he wanted more kids but why come he just didn't respect my wishes.

"Why are you sitting there like somebody died." Peaches said as she came and sat down next to me. The sound of my seven damn kids running through the house made me even more mad at the situation. The last thing we need is another baby.

"Nobody died. At least not yet. I'm about to kill your fucking son." I walked out of the kitchen and straight to the conference room. Momma Peaches was trying her best to stop me.

"Explain this shit Ka'Jaire." I threw the papers in his face and stood in front of him with my hands on my hips. He looked at the papers and threw them across the table.

"There's nothing to explain. As soon as I finish this meeting, we can discuss this. I told you to stop barging in here when the door is closed." He was pissing me off trying to play shit cool in front of his men.

"You're exactly right there is nothing discuss." I grabbed the papers and walked out of the room. When I got in the kitchen Momma Peaches, Gucci, and Dior were sitting around the table.

"What is going on Tahari?" Momma Peaches asked with an attitude

"Ka'Jaire paid the doctor off in Miami not to tie my tubes. Now I'm pregnant." I was so pissed off I grabbed me a glass and poured me some wine.

"I know damn well he didn't do no stupid shit like that.

"It's cool because I'm getting a fucking abortion." I had put the glass up to my mouth to drink but it was roughly knocked out of my hand by Thug.

"Bring your ass upstairs right now!" Thug yanked me up from the seat and I yanked away from his ass.

"Get your lying ass hands off of me. Just like there is nothing to explain, there is nothing to discuss. I don't want to talk about shit."

"You don't have a fucking a choice." He roughly grabbed me by the collar of my shirt and pushed me up the stairs.

"I know you better not put your fucking hands on her."

"I'm not going to hit Tahari. You already know that Ma but she better not hit me either."

As I walked inside my bedroom, I wiped the tears with the back of my hand. I was more hurt than mad. Thug came inside and he leaned up against the dresser. We were both quiet for an extended period of time until I decided to speak up.

"So, seven kids aren't enough for you?"

"I told you from the motherfucking jump that I want a house full of babies. Don't sit there and act like we never discussed this shit!" He was raising his voice and it was causing me to cry more.

"I'm not acting like we never discussed it but we agreed after I had the babies that we were done.

"I changed my mind. I wanted more kids." He grabbed a blunt from the nightstand and flamed it up.

"So, it's your way or nothing huh? Fuck what Tahari wants. It doesn't matter that I become overwhelmed. It doesn't matter that I'm sick as a dog the entire pregnancy. As long as I'm barefoot and pregnant. You're happy. In case you forgot I'm not your property. I'm your wife and I have a say so about my body and pussy. I don't want this baby and I'm getting an abortion. Whether you like it or not." I thought that Thug was going to snap the fuck out but instead he just walked out of the room without so much as a word. That meant he wanted to hit me so he walked away. I laid back on the bed and wondered if getting an abortion was the right thing to do. It wasn't that I couldn't handle another baby. In my heart I knew that we didn't need any more kids. Especially, now that Thug was Head of the Mob Family. Ka'Jaire Jr and Ka'Jairea are now seven years old. Kash and Kaine just made four years old. Ka'Jaiyah is three years old. Kaia and Kahari just made two. Being their mother is the best thing that ever could have happened to me. Raising them is no walk in the park. Thug doesn't understand that regardless of if he is around to help out. As the mother all the responsibilities fall back on me. A knock on my bedroom door brought me out of my thoughts.

"Come in."

"Hey. Are you okay?" Gucci asked as she stuck her head in the door.

"Not really. I really don't want this baby."

"It's going to be okay. I'm here for whatever decision you make. You're always here for me when I'm going through changes with King. It's only right I ride for you when you're going through shit with Thug."

"I know you do G. Did you talk to King yet?"

"I don't even want to look at him right now. I'm so fucking disgusted with him I don't know what the fuck to do."

"Go talk to him Gucci. He had no idea that bitch had a baby by him. None of us did. Just think about it. She hid that pregnancy from that man. I talked to him and he feels really bad about the shit. You're more than welcome to come back and spend the night over here with me. Plus I'll need some company in the guest room because it's going to be a minute before I lay next to Thug with his stupid ass." We both laughed.

"Okay. I'll go talk to King. I'm telling you now if he jump stupid with me, we're fighting and I mean that shit." Gucci walked out and the damn seven dwarfs walked in.

"Hey Momma. Daddy told us to come up here and give you a lot of kisses and hugs." Ka'Jaire Jr said as he climbed in bed and hugged and kissed me. I lifted Kaia and Kahari up on to the bed because they were having trouble getting up there.

"Mommy can I comb your hair?"

"Of course you can Baby girl?" Ka'Jariea loves playing in my hair. I'm surprised my shit hasn't fell out. Of course Kaine and Kash decided they want to jump and flip all in my bed. Ka'Jaiyah just climbed her spoil ass on my lap with her thumb in her mouth. Thug thought he was so slick he knew exactly what he was doing. He sent all of our kids up here to butter me up and make me change my mind about getting an abortion.

"Mommy I hope you have a girl this time. Then we will have four boys and four girls."

"Who told you I was having another baby Ka'Jariea."

"Daddy said you were giving him another seed. I heard him tell Uncle King and Dutch that babies are a beautiful thing and that you were giving him another baby to keep the family name going. I couldn't do nothing but shake my damn head. She just too grown for her own good. Thug knows he can't talk like that in front of her.

"What else did Daddy say Baby girl?"

"He told Uncle King that he fucked up big time."

"Ohhhh" All the kids said in unison because she had said a bad word.

"Watch your mouth!" I couldn't be mad at her because she was just telling me what she had heard. For the rest of the night I chilled back with my kids. I loved them all so much. I guess one more wouldn't hurt. Before you start talking about how stupid I am over Thug. If you had that nigga you would be stupid as hell too. You love Ka'Jaire "Thug" Kenneth as much as I do. I'm not keeping the baby because he wants it. I'm keeping it because God blessed me with another life and I wasn't even expecting it. Don't get it twisted I'm still pissed the fuck off at Thug for his sneaky and deceitful ass intentions. I'm not sure where we go from here. What Thug did to me was low down and dirty as hell. I really don't know how I'm supposed to deal with him going forward.

Chapter 27 - Thug

Coming to an Understanding

I honestly forgot that I had paid the doctor off not to tie Tahari's tubes. Right after she gave birth to Kaia and Kahari I told him to make her think she had in fact got her tubes tied. I now see how selfish I was back then. It was at a time when I wanted to keep Tahari barefoot and pregnant. All I wanted was for my baby to take care of home and raise our kids. She did that shit so well. Tahari is my life and the last thing I want her to do is stop trusting me. I just really got her trust back and I'm not trying to lose it. I fucked up big time. I really don't know what to say to her. I don't want her to get an abortion but if she does, I'll have to accept it.

"Are you straight Boss man?" King asked as we knocked back shots.

"Yeah. I'm cool. Just trying to figure out how I can make this shit up to my baby."

"There is nothing you can do to make shit up to her. That shit is real fucked up Ka'Jaire. I swear one of these days these girls are going get tired and leave ya asses. I've been talking to the ladies today and ya'll fucking up. I'm telling you right now when they leave your pathetic asses don't come calling me. I'm tired of helping ya'll make shit up to them girls. I advise all of you to get off your asses and make shit right with your better halves. I'll talk to ya'll later. I'm about to go Stepping with Gail and Mike. "Peaches kissed me on the forehead before she left out.

"Why she always got to be right? I'm about to head over here and put these kids to bed. I'll holla at you tomorrow when we make that move." King said as we dapped it up. I finished up the bottle and headed upstairs to face the music. Tahari was sitting up in bed reading as usual. I climbed in bed with her and snuggled up under her.

"What are you reading?

"Rozalyn 6. Don't come in here acting like shit is all good between because it's not. I'm mad as hell Ka'Jaire but I'm more hurt than anything. What you did was so sneaky and underhanded. What you did was no worse than a bitch stealing sperm and impregnating herself. If I had did some shit like that to you. You would have stop fucking with me without a second thought. You're truly a piece of fucking work." Tahari tried to push me off of her but I held on tight to her ass. I didn't care if a nigga had to beg like Keith Sweat.

"Baby, I'm so sorry. I wasn't thinking right. At the time all I wanted was for you to have my kids. You were acting like it was the worst thing in the world. That shit had me feeling some type of way. You're my wife and you not wanting to have my seeds really fucked me up in the head."

"Look around us Bae. We're not the typical married couple. We're running a Crime Family. It's bad enough we have seven kids that we have to shelter from this shit and from the world. Every day I pray that no one kidnap them or harms them trying to get to us. The last thing we need is more kids. Please know that carrying your babies is an honor. I just hate the morning sickness and the massive headaches. Plus, I'm scared I'm going to be pregnant with twins. Then we will have nine damn kids. Ain't nobody got time for that." I could see the worry in her eyes as she spoke.

"We can schedule an abortion first thing in the morning. You mean the world to me and I'm going to support whatever decision you make. I love you Ta-Baby." I grabbed her face and kissed her long and hard. I really didn't want her to get an abortion but I had to respect the fact that she no longer wanted kids.

"I love you too. I'm keeping the baby. The kids are all excited about me being pregnant. You knew what you were doing sending them upstairs too.

"I had to use my seven reinforcements." We both laughed and talked for the rest of the night. I was happy as hell she was keeping the baby. We both agreed that we would be done this time. She was hoping for one baby and I was praying for two. I wouldn't let her know that though. We had eventually fell asleep but was woke up with a call from Peaches saying that Mike had been shot at the lounge and we needed to get to the hospital. I could barely hear the shit that she was saying. I knew that Markese was about to crazy on whoever did the shit. I needed to be right there with my blood guns blazing.

Chapter 28- Momma Peaches

Here We Go Again

We were all having a good time at the Palm Tree Lounge. This was a place where all the old schoolers hung out at. Not the rowdy ass young crowd that likes to shoot and kill motherfucker if you step on their damn new shoes. I was on the floor stepping with an old friend from the neighborhood. Gail and Mike weren't that far from us stepping as well. Once the song was over, we headed back to our table.

"Well if it ain't Mike Jordan." We all looked up and it was this scandalous bitch Trixie.

"What's up Trixie?" Mike stuttered as spoke back. He looked as if he had seen a fucking ghost. We did as well because it had been years since we saw Trixie's lying and conniving ass.

"Get the fuck on somewhere with the bullshit. Ain't shit changed but the year and our ages. I will still stomp, beat, and drag your ass." Gail said as she stood up from her seat. I was ready for any and everything because this bitch Trixie was a real snake back in the day.

"Calm down baby there is no need for you to get all worked up." Mike grabbed Gail and she pulled away from his ass.

"Gail, I came over here to speak to the father of my children. He seems to have forgotten that he has two fully grown sons right now. You do remember King and Nasir, right?" Did this bitch just say what I think she said? Lord have mercy what is it with this baby momma and baby daddy drama.

"Trixie you know damn well I asked for a DNA test for them boys when they were babies. It was you who wanted me to pay you to get the test done. So, go on ahead away from him here trying to cause problems between me and my woman."

"You bitch!" Gail jumped over Mike and started whooping Trixie ass of course I started tagging her messy ass too. Gunshots rang out and I saw Mike slumped to the floor with a gunshot wound to his chest and stomach.

"Back the fuck up ladies. Before I put some hot shit in ya'll too. Looking good Gail baby. Long time no see." Sincere "Ox" Lennox was standing there holding the smoking gun. I should have known if Trixie was around, he wasn't too far behind.

"Why did you shoot him?" Gail was on the floor crying as she cradled Mike. He looked like he was struggling to breathe.

"What's good Peaches. I hear your sons are running shit now. Not to mention this bitch Trixie's sons and their little friend our fucking my daughters. Let them nigga's know I'm coming for what's mines. Which includes my girls and my streets." He whispered in my ear and him and Trixie backed out of the lounge. I knew it was about to be some shit. I immediately called Thug. The ambulance came and escorted Mike to the hospital. I was a nervous wreck as I rode to the hospital. When I walked into the emergency room. Thug, Sarge, Malik, Quaadir, Dro, Markese, Rahmeek, Killa, Boogie, King, Nasir and Dutch were all there waiting.

"Where is Gail at?" I noticed my sister wasn't in the family area. So, I started to panic.

"She's in the family room with the girls. What the hell happened Ma?"

"Thug, we need to sit down and talk. Let's go to the family room because this shit is crazy. We all walked to the family room and rushed to my sister's side. She kept staring at King and Nasir.

"They look like Markese and Mike. I never paid attention to it. Those are his son's. "Gail said and walked out of the family room. We tried to go after her but she stopped us letting us know that she needed time to herself.

"Okay look I'm going to get straight to the point. Ox shot Mike right after Trixie revealed that he is Nasir and King's father. Now I knew that Trixie had two sons back in the day but I had no clue it was King and Nasir. Ox ass was supposed to be dead. He pops up with Trixie at the lounge. He sending threats and all talking about he's coming for what's his. Meaning the streets and his daughters which happens to be Gucci, Chanel and Dior.

"So, it was our father who had Trixie and Lucky kidnap us?" Gucci asked.

"Wait a minute. Ya'll never said Trixie was in on that shit with Lucky."

"I'm sorry King. It just slipped my mind. So, much was going on when we came back.

"That means they killed Momma." Chanel said as she cried. Dior and Gucci was now crying as well. I felt sorry for these girls. They're mother was just killed at the hands of their psychotic ass father. Who we all thought were dead.

"Why couldn't her ass just stay the fuck away from us. We've been doing just fine without Trixie's ass. Mother or no mother her ass is dead and I mean that shit. She has never been a fucking mother but has the nerve to be messy and reveal who are father is. She wasn't doing that shit for me or Nasir. All that was a part of her sick twisted ass game. That nigga Ox is a dead motherfucker as well." King was visibly upset as he spoke. Nasir just sat there in deep thought.

"Don't trip King. We've been family for a minute now anyway. I always wanted little brother's to boss around and tell them what to do anyway." Markese said as he hugged both Nasir and King.

"I can't believe I have three brothers now. Ya'll owe me a gift for being away so long." Aja got up and gave them a hug as well. We all stood and smiled at them. It was the only bright spot at the moment.

"He's going to be okay. I just talked to the doctor and the bullets missed all vital organs." Gail rushed in and was hugging Markese and Aja.

"Welcome to the family King and Nasir." Gail turned around and hugged them as well. She was taking this better than I expected. Gail wasn't fooling me though. As soon as Mike gets well, she going to lay all into his ass. I know I would fucking with that thot Trixie. I had to get out of here and get me some damn Patron. I had enough drama for one day.

Chapter 28 - Dior

Consequences

After I lit the match and set my house on fire. I knew that there would be consequences behind my actions. Things would never be the same between us. Too much had been said and our actions were unacceptable. Being kidnapped and knowing that my father had a part in it really fucked me up in the head. Life for me has been fucked up since Dutch killed our baby. I know that Dutch hates me and wants to whoop my ass real good for burning up the house. The only thing that's sparing me from that ass whooping is all the bullshit that's going on. He hasn't said a word to me. He just stares at me with his cold black eyes. He wants to murder my ass. I want to say something to him but my best bet is to sit back be quiet and shut the fuck up. We were all in deep thought as we waited for King and Nasir to finish visiting with Mike.

I observed Dutch constantly texting and checking his phone. Abruptly, he jumped up and headed out of the family room. I don't know why but I knew some shit was up. Of course, my nosy ass just had to get up and follow him.

"Where are you going, Dior?" I heard Chanel say as I rushed out of the door.

She, Gucci, and Tahari were following me. I looked around the Emergency Room and saw Natavia at the nurses' station holding her stomach. Dutch was standing beside her rubbing her back. The receptionist got on the intercom and called for a wheelchair attendant to escort Natavia to Labor and Delivery. I hadn't even noticed the bulge in her stomach at the restaurant or back at the house when we were fighting. I didn't know I was crying until I felt the wetness on my face.

"Please tell me this big bitch ain't pregnant by you." Hurt dripped from the words I spoke.

"What does it look like? Unlike you, I'm the bitch he wants a baby with. Tell he that this is your baby."

"Shut your stupid ass up, Natavia. I swear you can be so fucking stupid at times."

"Wow! So, she gets to keep her baby and mine was murdered?"

"Really, Dutch? How could you do her like that?" Tahari said as she tried to pull me away.

"No disrespect, Boss Lady, but fuck Dior. Did she tell ya'll that she was cheating on me with Lucky. Then she burnt my fucking Range and house to the ground. Dior ain't innocent in all this. She made her bed and now her ass has to lay in it."

Dutch walked right past us with the attendant that was pushing Natavia in the wheelchair. She had the biggest smirk on her face.

"Oh hell no! Dutch, you a bitch ass nigga for this shit!" Chanel said trying to go after him.

"Fuck him. Let that nigga go ahead on. She's stressed out enough and she don't need this shit right now," Gucci said as she hugged me. Tahari and Chanel followed suit. I just stood there speechless with tears falling down my face.

****

It had been a couple of hours since I left the hospital and I was emotional wreck. As I sat on the floor in one of the spare bedrooms of Thug and Tahari's guesthouse, I contemplated my life and if it was worth living. I had nothing. My mother was dead, my relationship with Dutch was dead, and everyone around me was happy. It seemed like I would never get my happened. That shit just wasn't in the cards for me.

The doctor had prescribed some Xanax after I lost the baby. Depression was kicking my ass. I never even used one pill because I knew how addictive they could be. I weighed my pros and cons about my life and my cons came out on top. I decided to take the pills. I didn't want to hurt anymore. I just wanted to go to sleep forever so that I could numb all of the pain. One by one, I took all the pills in the bottle.

Eventually, I drifted off into the best sleep that I had in a long time. I could hear Dutch calling my name over and over again. I could also hear Gucci crying. Their voices started to fade away and I could no longer hear them. I had found my happy place and it felt wonderful. Then all of sudden I could hear my mother saying the words weak and pathetic over and over in my head. For a moment, I was headed towards peace and serenity. My mother's voice accompanied with beeping sounds woke me up from my semi-conscious state.

I slowly opened my eyes and tried to focus on my surroundings. The familiar beeping sounds let me know I was in the hospital. I guess I wasn't successful in killing myself. I looked over and there was a police officer sitting in the room by the door. I tried to move but I couldn't because I was handcuffed.

"Why the fuck am I handcuffed?"

"Calm down ma'am. You've been placed under arrest. Once you're released, they'll tell you what your charges are."

I just laid in the bed and tried to think of why I was under arrest. Not long after Chanel and Gucci arrived.

"Please get me out of here."

"We can't, Dior. You're under arrest for that shit that went down at your crib. Plus, you tried to kill yourself. Why would you do something like that?" Chanel said as she stood over the bed. Gucci was looking at me with sympathetic eyes.

"My life is all fucked up. That's why I did it. Just make sure you get me a lawyer. Sooner or later I know that they will be taking me in to custody soon."

"Dutch already got you one."

"He presses charges on me and then gets me a lawyer. Where they do that at?"

"Actually, Natavia pressed charges. Dutch is really pissed off about it," Gucci said.

"I don't care. All this is his fault and I never want to see him again."

"Okay ladies. You have to go now. The police officer said.

I wasn't about to cry about going to jail. If I was going to get some time then so be it. I had no regrets about burning that motherfucker down. I would do again in a minute. Gucci and Chanel looked like they were about to cry and I couldn't have that right now.

"Don't cry. I'm okay. I'll call ya'll once I get situated."

We all hugged each other and they left. Not long after I was transported to the county jail. I had been charged with arson, assault, and two counts of attempted murder. I wasn't expecting the attempted murder charges. I wondered if I would get a bond. If I did, I had every intention on killing the bitch Natavia, pregnant and all.

Chapter 29 - King

We Are One

It's great feeling to know that I have a father and a son. I would rather it had been under different circumstances. Despite it all, I'm grateful. It's always been just me and Nasir. Having a father has never even crossed our minds. It's crazy how in a matter of days our family has grown tremendously. The events that have transpired over the last couple of days have me fucked up in the head. Trixie's involvement in all of this has me fuming. Gucci, Chanel, and Dior have never done anything to her. She was doing all that shit for some nigga. I'm not surprised though. Dick has always come before anything in her life. I hate that I have to kill her but she brought harm to the love of my life and that shit cannot fly. I'm killing anything that threatens the empire I'm trying to build.

I loved how KJ and Imani acted as if they had known each other forever. We were now back at our home. I have armed men standing guard outside. I got some shit ready for whoever got the balls to step on my property.

The movie *In Too Deep* played on the projection screen in my man cave. The Kush blunts accompanied with the Patron I had been drinking had a nigga high as hell. The movie was on but I wasn't even watching it. My mind was on Gucci and where our relationship was headed. The last thing I wanted was for us to end up like Dior and Dutch. The crazy part about it is that they're the reason the rest of us are together. I know that Dutch loves Dior and she loves him. Hopefully, they will stop this shit and get it together. I don't trust the bitch Natavia and I made it perfectly clear I don't want her around me. I can tell that she's a snake. Gucci and I haven't had a chance to talk about anything because she refuses to talk about it. I refuse to kiss her ass and get her to talk to me.

I haven't done anything wrong and I refuse to let her make me feel like I have. I just decided to give her some space until she was ready to talk. In the meantime, I needed to have a clear head when I killed these motherfuckers.

****

I woke up the next morning to the smell of breakfast cooking. I had fallen asleep on the couch in my man cave. I sat up and handled my personal hygiene before heading to the kitchen. A niggas stomach was in his back. Gucci, Imani, and KJ were sitting at the table eating breakfast when I entered the kitchen.

"That's how ya'll do me, huh?"

"Good Morning. Your food is on the stove," Gucci said as she continued to eat without looking up at me.

"Good Morning. I appreciate it." I tried my luck and bent down to kiss her. Surprisingly, she kissed me back. I grabbed my plate and joined them at the table.

"Can we go to the mall today, Daddy?" Imani asked with a mouth full of pancakes.

"Didn't I already tell your ass no. I told you to stop doing that shit." I looked at Gucci liked she had two heads. I really hate it when Gucci curses at our daughter.

"Not today. If you want to, we can make it a family day. I'll let you and your brother pick the movies and eat whatever you want."

"Yayyy!" they both screamed in excitement.

"Are you going to have family day with us, Gucci?" KJ asked with the biggest smile on his face. I looked at Gucci and waited for her to answer. It really pissed me off that she was trying to ignore him and act as if she didn't hear what he had said.

"Mommy, my brother is talking to you."

I watched as Gucci turned her nose up and rolled her eyes at our daughter. That was it. I couldn't take it anymore. I got up from the table and slammed my whole plate in the sink.

"Bring your ass upstairs," I said low enough that only she could hear. She got up from the table and followed behind me slowly. As soon as we got inside, I pushed her against the wall.

"I know you're in your feelings, but don't you ever treat my kids like that. I know you don't like KJ but he's just a kid. In case you forgot, he has no mother. I can't believe you cursed at Imani like that. If this how you're going to act then we can call this quits right now. I have enough on my plate with trying to protect ya'll. I ain't got time for the shit that you're doing. If his being here is too much, I'll get us a hotel room."

"It's not about him being here." Tears were streaming down her face. I wiped her tears with my thumb and led her to the bed. I sat her down and pulled her on my lap.

"Then what is it baby. Talk to your man."

"It's everything, King. My mother is dead. My father is alive and trying to hurt me. Your mother is hurting both of us. My sister tried to kill herself and now she's fighting for her freedom, and we have a new addition to our family. I'm sorry but I'm overwhelmed and I don't know what to do. Please forgive me for my behavior towards your son. My heart is hurting really bad. I always wanted to give you your first born son."

"I swear on my life. I didn't know anything about him. Shortly after you left Samina showed up with him. I took one look at him and I knew that he was mine. I killed her ass and I had no other choice but to bring him with me. From what he told me, she punished him for being my son. That shit tugged at my heart. She went out of her way to hide him from me but made sure to tell him about me and Imani. He's been on cloud nine since he's been with us. I can't make him suffer any more than he already has. I grew up without a mother or a father. That shit will not happen to him or Imani as long as I have air in my body. You, of all people, know that I have a weakness for kids. I understand if you want to walk away.

"Who said anything about leaving you? That's the furthest thing from my mind. Lord willing, I want to spend the rest of my life with you. I love you more than anything in this world. I'll be a good mother to KJ and even better wife to you."

Hearing Gucci say those words made me feel good as hell. I could now focus on handling Trixie and Ox.

"I'm so happy you're riding for a nigga. How would you feel if I sent you and the kids to Disney World for about a week?"

"Hell no! You think you're slick. I want in on this shit. I already told you I'm riding beside you. So, what's the plan? Plus, what the fuck we look like going on a trip without you. Once all this is over, we're going on a family trip."

"You got my dick harder than a motherfucker right now." I had to adjust my shit because Gucci had a nigga about to erupt right then and there.

"Oh yeah. It's been a minute since I had a taste of him. Let me go get the kids situated and I'll be right back."

I got undressed and laid in bed my eyes darted over to the dresser. I remembered the ring I had picked out for her. With everything that was going on, I never got a chance to propose to her.

"KJ is so overprotective of Imani," Gucci said as she walked in the room and started to get undressed.

"Yeah, he loves her already," I said as I wrapped my arms around Gucci's waist and placed soft kisses on her neck.

"I love you so much, G. I can't imagine my life without you. You're my air. Without you, I can't breathe. My life is nothing without you in it. I guess what I'm trying to say is, will you marry me?"

"Ahhhhh!" Gucci screamed as I slid the yellow canary diamond on her finger.

"Oh my God! King, it's so beautiful. I love you so much baby. I have to call Chanel and Tahari and tell them I'm getting married." Gucci was kissing me all over my lips and face.

"Wait a minute, G. I thought you was about to kiss the crown." I pointed down to my hard-on.

"I'm sorry, baby. I have to call my girls. I have a wedding to plan, baby. Call Thug and the crew and tell them to get ready for our wedding. All white everything."

Gucci ran out of the room full speed ahead. I sat down on the bed and smiled. Just knowing my baby was happy made me happy. She deserved nothing but happiness and I was going to die trying to make her the happiest woman alive. She deserved that and more.

Chapter 30 - Gucci

A Sisters Love

I can't believe King proposed to me. I never thought this day would come. I've been staring at my ring for hours. I think I love it more than King's ass. My baby did the damn thing when he copped this.

After cooking dinner all I wanted to do was take a long hot bath and take in everything. Thoughts of my mother flooded my mind as I soaked in the tub. She would be ecstatic knowing that Chanel and I would be getting married. I also know that she would be pissed off about Dior sitting in jail for burning down her own damn house. I laughed a little as I shed tears of sadness and joy. You only get one mother. When she's gone, there's no coming back from that. I know she's at peace now.

The idea of having another kid in the house has me all unsure of my feelings and actions. I have to get used to the fact that King has a son. I'm so jealous. I wanted to give him his first-born son. Samaya is a pain in my ass from the grave. KJ is a well-behaved little boy. I know that he has to get used to being around me as well. I love kids so I would never mistreat him or make him feel uncomfortable.

Dior's bond hearing is in the morning and I pray she gets bond. I'm going crazy knowing that she is in that dirty ass jail. She needs to be at home with her family getting her life together. She trying to kill herself has me all fucked up in the head. I'm just grateful she's okay. I don't know what I would have done if I had lost her too.

****

"I hope Dior gets a bond. I'm going crazy thinking about her being in jail," Chanel said as we rode to the courthouse.

"You and me both. I still can't believe Dutch's ass."

"Fuck him. I have no words for his ass. It's his fault she's going through all this shit."

"The last thing I want to talk about is Dutch. What's going on with you? How are Nasir and the baby?" I had to change the subject because the mention of Dutch's name made my ass ache.

"They're doing good. Nasir is getting stronger and stronger. I would prefer for him not to go out of the house but he insists getting out in these streets with King. Baby Nasir is getting fatter and he is spoiled as hell. Nasir carries him around all day and sleeps with him on his chest. He is such a crybaby. He wants to be held all day long. I can't even get mad at Nasir for how he is spoiling him. Getting shot fucked him up. Not to mention this shit with Trixie. He keeps apologizing about what she did to us. I keep telling him it's not his fault. They had no idea the bitch was fucked up in the head."

"King refuses to discuss it. He said he's killing her and Ox. End of discussion."

"I'll be glad when they get their asses. I'm ready to get back to normal life."

"I know that's right, lil sis."

We found a parking space and headed inside. I was fuming when I saw Natavia walking towards the courtroom. As soon as she saw us, she started rubbing her stomach.

"Bitch, please! Don't get it twisted. I'll whoop a pregnant bitch ass." Chanel said and we both started laughing.

"That's why the bitch is in jail now and I'm going to see to it that she stays in there. She has to go. Dutch and I are going to be together. We don't want her ruining my happy family. I'll send you invitations to our baby shower and our wedding."

"Fuck outta here. I'll send flowers to your funeral, bitch. That's where you're headed if you keep fucking with my sister."

I pushed the bitch out of my way and took a seat. This chick had some real issues. The judge was a bitch. She was playing no games. She was giving out No Bonds left and right. Finally, it was Dior's turn and I wanted to cry when they brought her out. Chanel and I grabbed each other's hands. We breathed a sigh of relief when she gave her three hundred thousand dollar bond. I looked over at Natavia and she was seeing red. I couldn't do shit but laugh at her dumb ass.

"Let's go call Dutch so we can let him know what her bond is," Chanel said as we made our way out of the courthouse.

"Do you think he's going to bond her out?"

"Yeah. He called me this morning and told me to call him as soon as we found out what her bond is."

"That's good to know." I was so anxious to get home and cook dinner for my sister. I want her at home with me. She might protest but I'm the big sister. It's time for me to step up and take on the motherly role with these two crazy sisters of mine.

Chapter 31-Dior

Feels Good To Be Free

Walking out of that damn jail felt good as hell. I exhaled as I locked eyes with Dutch who was standing beside a new white Range. I rolled my eyes and walked right past his ass. We were over so there really was no need for us to even speak.

"I know you see me standing here. Get your ass in the truck." He grabbed my arm and I yanked it away.

"Shouldn't you be somewhere with your baby momma?"

"Fuck that bitch. I don't even think that baby is mine anyway."

"Is that supposed to make me feel better?"

I was standing in front of him with my arms folded across my chest. He pulled me in close to him so that I was leaning up against his body. He moved some strands of hair from my face and stared at me for a couple of seconds.

"I thought I lost you when I found you on the floor like that."

His eyes looked like they were watering. I put my head down in shame as it came to me that my dumb ass tried to kill myself.

"I really have to go and get cleaned up. Have a nice life, Dominique." I tried walking away but he was holding on to me tight as hell.

"Come back to my hotel room. I picked up a couple of items for you. I know you ain't got shit since you burned it all up.

I laughed a little because I forgot all about that. I reluctantly got inside. Who was I kidding? I really didn't have anywhere to go. I know that my sisters would have welcomed me with open arms but they had their families to take care of. I really didn't want to be a burden. We drove in silence the majority of the ride to the hotel.

"Do you love her?"

"I love you and only you. She don't mean shit to me. I never should have start fucking with her. I should have been at home trying to fix my relationship with you. I pushed you into the arms of that nigga."

"I never had sex with him. We only went out to eat a couple of times." I had cut him off in mid-sentence.

"It doesn't even matter. Had I not put my hands on you to begin with we would be enjoying becoming parents. Instead, we're hurting each other. I'm sorry from the bottom of my heart. Seeing you lying on the floor like that fucked me up in the head."

I looked over and watched as tears streamed down his face. I leaned over and wiped them with my hands.

"I'm sorry I scared you. I was at the lowest point in my life. I didn't have you anymore and that shit hurt. It's cool though. I know it's over between us. My heart will heal and I'll get the happiness that I deserve."

"That's the thing Dior. I don't want to be without you. Can we please work this shit out? I need you, Ma. I promise that I'll get my shit together."

"I can't answer that right now. I'm not sure I can handle you having a baby with someone else. Can we talk about it later? I just want to get to the hotel and get cleaned up. I smell horrible and I feel dirty as hell."

"Yeah, you're right. I can smell your ass over here."

We both laughed. That made me feel good. I couldn't remember the last time we shared a laugh. As soon as we made it to the hotel. I called my sisters and let them know I was in the Presidential Suite at the Fairmont.

"I ran you some bath water. You should get in before it gets cold."

"Thank you."

I walked inside the bathroom and got undressed. The tub was huge. I got inside the water and moaned in pleasure. That bed in the jail did a number on my body. Once I bathed and showered, I put on one of Dutch's shirts and climbed in the bed. I pulled the covers up over my body and laid there looking up at the ceiling.

Can Dutch really make this shit up to me? Do I even want his ass after all that he has put me through? I fell asleep with Dutch on my mind.

****

I was having the best wet dream ever. I was riding beautiful waves of ecstasy. I felt as though I was having an outer body experience. The feeling of me pissing on myself brought me out of my wet dream real quick. I was wet as hell. My eyes fluttered as I was able to focus on what was really going on. I couldn't believe my eyes. I tried to move Dutch's head from in between my legs.

"Don't fight me, Dior." Dutch gently pushed my hands away.

"Please stop, Dutch. We can't do this." Dutch was sucking and biting all on my pussy lips. That shit was driving me crazy.

"Your pussy tastes so good. I missed this shit so much."

He stood up and wiped his mouth with the back of his hand. He was naked as the day he was born. Dick was standing tall as the Sears Tower. It had been so long since I took a really good look at his body. He was cut the fuck up. His abs were chiseled to perfection. He had worked up a sweat putting in work on my pussy. My mouth watered as he stroked his manhood.

"Can I make love to you, Dior?"

I nodded my head. I would have said yes to anything as I took in his sexy ass physique. He lifted each one of my feet and sucked on my toes one by one. Dutch was definitely on one tonight. He was licking toes and eating pussy. Dutch rarely did that. I made sure to take full advantage of his ass. He climbed in between my legs and stroked my wet pussy with his dick. In one swift motion, he pushed his entire dick inside of me. It had been a minute and that shit hurt like hell. I winced in pain as I sank my nails in his back as deep as they could go.

"All I want is another chance to make you happy. Can I make you happy again?" He was deep stroking my ass with everything inside of him. I was on the verge of tears as he fucked the shit out of me. Dutch was sucking and biting all over my neck.

"Marry me, Dior. I want to spend the rest of my life without you. Tell me you'll marry me."

"Yes, Dominique, I'll marry you," I answered in the heat of the moment.

I wasn't quite sure that I really wanted to marry him but what the fuck did I have to lose? The last thing I wanted was seeing him with Natavia. I had put in too many years and tears to lose him to a bitch who couldn't hold a candle to me. I already know that she's the one that pressed charges against me. Fuck her and her baby. If she wanted Dutch, she was going to have to take him from me and I wasn't going down without a fight.

Not long after we were both coming at the same time. The feeling of me creaming all over his dick and him letting all his seeds loose inside of me had me shaking like a leaf. He lay on top of me for a minute. I felt him grab my hand and slide a ring on it. He rose up off of me and went to the bathroom. I sat up in bed looking at the biggest princess cut diamond I had ever seen.

"You like that, baby? If you don't, I can get you another one that makes you happier."

"It's fine, Dutch." I sounded so unenthusiastic.

"Are you sure you want to marry me?" he asked as he rubbed his hand across my face.

"Yes, I want to marry you but you have to be completely done with Natavia. I don't give a fuck if her baby is yours. That bitch is a distant memory or I will make her one and your ass too."

"You got it. All I want is you. That's my motherfucking word. I love you so much."

"I love you too."

He crawled back in bed and we made love to for the rest of the night. I didn't know what the future held but I could only hope for the best.

The next morning I woke up to the sound of someone beating on the hotel room door. Dutch was knocked out. I got up to answer the door thinking that it was the hotel staff.

"So, this why that nigga ain't answering the phone for me. Where the fuck is he?" Natavia yelled as she tried to push pass me.

"Bitch, if you don't back the fuck up. He's sleep and he's had a long night."

"You're so funny to me. That nigga only want you because your weak ass tried to kill yourself. Get the fuck out of my way before I beat your ass."

Natavia was trying her best to push past me but I wasn't budging. I was praying her ass swung on me so that I could whoop her ass. Before I could respond, hotel security was swarming us. Dutch had woke up as well.

"What the fuck is going on?" Dutch said as he walked towards us naked as hell.

"I can't fucking believe you, Dutch! I was just here with you two nights ago. Now this bitch is here. Did you fuck her?" Natavia was going crazy. I just stood by the door looking at her ass like the crazy bitch she was.

"Get this bitch out of here before I kill her ass." Dutch was walking towards her and I jumped in front of him and pushed him back.

"Fuck her. Let them escort her away. We have a wedding to plan."

I kissed him and made sure to flash my ring. I was being messy but so what. I needed to give that bitch a taste of her own medicine. Dutch wrapped his arms around me and we kissed each other.

"I'm killing you and her ass. Watch me work. I've been here when that bitch wouldn't even talk to your ass. Yesterday, you hated her ass. Now today you're marrying this bitch? I'm the one carrying your baby, nigga, not her pyromaniac ass. Did you forget she burnt your fucking house down? If it's the last thing I do I'm going to get you back. Bitch ass nigga!" Security now had her by the waist escorting her away from the hotel room.

"This is the shit I refuse to deal with. You need to put her ass in her place. She's too damn ignorant for me." I walked into the room and started getting dressed to meet up with Chanel and Dior.

"So, you're mad at me now?"

"No, I'm not mad at you Dutch. I will not tolerate that bitch popping up and showing her ass. I will kill that bitch before I let her think it's okay to disrespect me. Now get dressed so that we can go kick it with our family. It's a new us and we're going to stay on the right track."

I kissed him on the lips and walked into the bathroom to finish getting ready. I had my doubts about our relationship but I wouldn't let him know that. It was game the fuck on. All bets were off. His ass better be one hundred percent sure being married to me was what he really wanted. I would kill his ass dead before the thought of me killing myself ever crossed my mind again.

*****

"I need to check on some shit for King. As soon as I'm finished, we'll head over to their crib. Are you cool with that?"

"Yeah, I'm cool with it."

We rode through the hood picking up money from the traps and just checking on things. As I rode in the passenger seat, I paid attention to what Dutch was doing. For some reason I felt like I should watch him as he worked. I also was paying attention to my surroundings. As we drove past the projects, I saw a man that bore striking resemblance to my father. I shook Dutch to get his attention because the man looked like he was in a heated conversation with Natavia on the sidewalk. The smack he delivered to her face made her fall hard as hell.

"I'm going to kill this bitch ass nigga and that bitch!" Dutch grabbed his gun and was getting ready to park. He was trying to get out but I grabbed his arm before he could exit.

"No. Let's just watch and see what's going on."

We sat and watched as he yanked her ass off of the ground and pushed her inside the back seat of a black Chrysler 300. Trixie strutted out of a building and got in the front seat. They pulled off and we followed. Thirty minutes later, they pulled in front of the same building where my sisters and I were held.

"This is the house they brought us to when we were kidnapped."

"So, this is where they've been all this time."

I watched in awe as Ox yanked Natavia out of the car and slapped her around a couple of more times. I felt a little bad for her. Trixie got out and tried to stop Ox from hitting her. He ended up backhanding her. She got back in the car quick as hell. Ox got in the car as well. Natavia walked up the stairs crying and inside the house.

"What are we going to do now?" I asked as Dutch drove away.

"I need to get with King and Nasir. Their mother is involved in this shit and I know they want in on killing Ox."

"What if they disappear?"

"They're not going anywhere. They have gotten comfortable."

When we arrived at King's house, Nasir and Chanel were there as well. King, Nasir, and Dutch went to talk in private. I had a feeling they were about to ditch us and not let us in on shit. I had a trick for them though. My sisters and I deserved some get back and I knew just how to get it. They would thank us later.

Chapter 32 - Natavia

I Didn't Choose This Life

I couldn't believe that this was my life had come to me. I needed Dutch so bad. He was supposed to my escape from all this bullshit. I never asked to be brought into this world. My parents Ox and Trixie should be the poster child for bad ass parents. Their whole lives revolve around scheming, robbing, stealing, and hurting people to get ahead. All this shit that's going on had been one big ass scheme to get Dior, Chanel, and Gucci back to Las Vegas so that they can join me on his stable. Ox wants his daughters to sell pussy for him. I had no idea they were my sisters. I also had no idea Nasir and King were my brothers This is some fucked up shit.

From a young age, Trixie groomed me for the day I would join her and the rest of them stupid bitches on the track. No girl wants to live like this. Ox was my father so I had no choice. I've been working for him since I was thirteen.

When we first arrived here a couple of months ago, we already had a plan to start back up the drug business that Ox used to have back in the day. Lucky was the only one on the streets who agreed to help Ox. He had a vendetta against King, Nasir, and Dutch but he never told me what it was. Ox was thinking that he could just pop his supposed dead ass back here and take over. Little did he know, the streets already were taken by some nigga named Thug.

In the midst of trying to find out who Thug was, Trixie found out that her son, King, was running the drug operation. You would think she would want to see her long lost sons after abandoning them. No, she was ready to bring harm to them. That's when I found out they were my brothers. Sincere got inside her and they began scheming on taking their own kids down. That whole scene with her bumping into Nasir's car crossing the street was a fucking set up. She had found out about his routine and that's how she ended up in the street at the same time he was driving.

Sincere is the mastermind behind all of this shit. He made her go to Candy's house and kill her. She was laughing so hard after she pulled the trigger. They found out that Candy had been trying to find info on them. They had to kill her before she fucked up their plans. I should have run far away from her ass right then and there but where the fuck would I go? I don't have a pot to piss in or a window to throw it out of. That's where Dutch came in. From the moment I laid eyes on him, I had to have him all to myself. My daddy told me to finesse him and learn everything I needed to know about him. I knew that he loved Chili's and he ate there damn near every day. Ox hollered at the manager and he hired me on the spot. Instead, I got some of that good ass dick and I've been lost ever since.

I found out I was pregnant when I first came to Chicago. There was no way I was pregnant by Dutch but he didn't have to know that. Most likely I was pregnant by Ox. I stayed in his bed more than Trixie. That's why he's been whooping my ass. He knows I'm in love with Dutch and he hates how I've been behaving over him.

All this shit is Dior's fault. All she had to do was die when she tried to kill herself. I was going to be with Dutch and we were going to raise a family and be happy together. I just knew he was done with her after she burned down the house. Instead, he started whooping on my ass like I had done something wrong.

I died a thousand times when I got to his hotel room. He was ignoring my calls and texts. Something told me he was with that bitch. I got my confirmation when she answered the door with his shirt on. I acted a stone cold fool until I was escorted out of the hotel.

I want to kill the bitch Dior myself. She made it a habit of always calling me fat. I hated that shit. Dutch loves all my curves. I'm a perfect size eighteen with a voluptuous ass and nice rack to go with it. My confidence is through the roof. Skinny bitches hate to give plus-sized women their respect. Little do they know; their niggas love plus-sized bitches. I've been the other bitch plenty of times. Bitches' eyes got big ass saucers when they find out their husband or man had been cheating on them with a big bitch. That's why I walk with an extra switch in my hip. These bitches hate it but their niggas loves it.

I can't take this shit anymore. I need to get the fuck out of here before Trixie and Ox come back. Fuck them and fuck Dutch. I needed to get my life right if I wanted to prosper. I'm a good person. I was just raised by some scheming motherfuckers.

"Going somewhere, bitch?" a voice said from behind me.

I turned around. It was Dior, Chanel, and Gucci. Dior walked towards me and hit me across the head with a gun, knocking me out instantly.

Chapter 33 - Gucci

Off With Her Head

King, Dutch, and Nasir are going to kick our asses for this shit. I couldn't believe we had kidnapped the bitch Natavia. We carried her heavy ass from the house and put her in the back of my truck. We went to the storage space and tied her to a chair.

"Damn, Dior! How hard did you hit the bitch?" Chanel asked as she slapped her around a couple of times. Blood was also dripping from the gash in the back of her head.

"I didn't mean to knock her ass out. I just wanted to shut the bitch up before she started popping off at the mouth," Dior said as she took a long pull from the blunt and handed it to me. I took a long pull and handed it to Chanel. I found an old bucket, filled it up with cold water, and threw it on her ass.

"Ahhhhhh!" she screamed, looking like she was in a daze. We laughed hard as hell because she looked like she had seen a ghost.

"Wake the fuck up, sleeping beauty," Dior said as she stood in front of Natavia blowing weed smoke in her face.

"What the fuck you bitches want?"

"Watch your motherfucking mouth! We're asking the questions." Chanel smacked her so hard in the mouth that blood started to come from her lips.

"So, you were in on this shit with Ox and Trixie, huh?" Dior asked as she started going inside her purse.

"Of course I was that's what good little girls do. They listen to their parents."

"Girl get the fuck out of here. They are not your parents. You're a lying ass bitch!" Chanel said as she flicked her ashes on her.

"I don't have a reason to lie to you bitches. How does it feel knowing your sister fucked your man and is pregnant by him?

"Shut the fuck up. You retarded ass bitch!

Kill yourself. Oops! I forgot you already tried that. You know what; you're an unsuccessful ass bitch. You suck at trying to kill yourself and you suck at being a good woman to Dutch. Let's keep it one hundred, Dior. This has nothing to do with my mother or my father. You have me here because of my relationship with Dutch. I loved fucking your man. It was something about the way he hit my shit from the back. The feeling of his massive hands smacking my ass had me creaming all over his dick. You better hope he likes fucking you after he had this pussy. Your mouth better work miracles. I was trying to suck the skin off his dick."

This bitch is truly out of her fucking mind. Her laughing was maniacal. I could tell she was getting under Dior's skin.

"Do you think you're hurting me by running off at the mouth about you and Dutch? I could care less. You were something to do when there was nothing to do. You tried to suck the skin off the dick and you still didn't end up with him. Oh yeah, he knows that baby ain't his."

"Your ass is mad because I'm about to have his baby and you're not. Jealousy is not cute on you, sweetie."

"I'm so sick of this bitch's mouth. Please shut her the fuck up," Chanel said as she got up and kicked her ass out of the chair. She lay on the floor in pain for a minute before I lifted her ass back up into sitting position.

"I'm glad you said that, Chanel. I have just the thing to shut her rat ass up." I watched as Dior pulled a couple of boxes of rat poison from her purse.

"Rat bitches like you need to be silenced. Hold that bitch's mouth open so I can feed her ass."

"Get the fuck away from me with that shit!" Natavia started to squirm and fight but she was no match for us holding her mouth open and Dior force-feeding her rat poison.

"Now let that marinate, bitch!" Dior said as she poured the last of the rat poison down her throat.

We sat there for hours and watched as she gagged and vomited. I wanted to vomit my damn self as her ass foamed at the mouth.

The sound of the doors opening made us jump. I just knew it was the police about to take our asses to jail for murder. I kind of wished it was the police because the look on King, Dutch, and Nasir's faces had us shitting bricks

Chapter 34 - King

Shit Just Got Real

As I walked into our storage unit, all I could do was shake my head. Gucci, Chanel, and Dior were standing in the middle of the room looking like they had just got caught with their hands in the cookie jar. Once I got closer, I became heated at the sight Natavia. I wasn't mad because they had did her in. I was mad because they did the shit without permission. I didn't have to say a word to Gucci. I had every intention on ripping her a new asshole when all this was over.

"Bring their asses in here and tie them up next to that bitch!" Dutch said to our men who had Trixie and Ox.

"So, y'all just doing what the fuck ya'll want to do, huh?" Nasir asked he got in Chanel's face.

"We had to help Dior," Chanel said, looking scared as hell.

"Shut the fuck up. I'll deal with your ass when we get home." Chanel wanted to say something back but she knew better than to speak at the moment.

"I think it's real fucked up that you went behind my back when I specifically told you that I would handle the shit," Dutch said to Dior as he started rolling up his sleeves.

"I had to get her ass myself and I'm not apologizing for it either."

"No one asked your smart mouth ass to apologize. I'm just saying you should have run it past me first."

Dutch kissed and Dior and turned around and hit Ox ass so hard that teeth flew from his mouth "Ya'll just gon' stand there and let these niggas hurt your daddy? I came back here to give ya'll a better life in Las Vegas with me. My stable needs three bad bitches like ya'll. Looking just like that bitch Candy. How was her funeral by the way?"

He had an evil smirk on his face and I was ready to kill his ass right then and there. My mother was just sitting in the chair with her head held down. I prayed that she felt ashamed of herself. I looked over at Gucci, Chanel, and Dior. They were all crying. Seeing them hurting hurt me and I wasn't about to let no motherfucking body hurt them again.

"Yo! Nasir grab the aluminum bats from that closet," I said and stood behind the chair my mother was sitting in.

"Ya'll still want to put in work?" I asked Gucci, Chanel, and Dior.

I was surprised when they said yeah. I thought that nigga Ox had broke them but he had just fucked up. I was actually hoping they said yes. It was sad to know that our parents went to great lengths to hurt us. We were all learning a valuable lesson that no one was to be trusted, not even the motherfuckers that created or birthed you. Dutch, Nasir, and I already knew that. This shit was new for the girls but this experience would have them on point and ready for whatever going forward.

"Grab a bat and whoop that nigga then."

Nasir handed each of them a bat. He and Dutch stood back and let them put in work on Ox. Gucci delivered a blow to Ox's head that opened his shit like a watermelon. I looked over at Trixie and she was crying with her head hung low

"Hold your head up and watch them kill that nigga because your ass is next."

I roughly yanked her head up and made her watch them pulverize his ass. Once I saw that they were getting tired, I gestured for Dutch and Nasir to take over. I joined in. On cue, we pulled our nines from our waist and emptied our clips in his ass. Dutch gave Natavia two dome shots. I was glad because all that damn gurgling and foaming at the mouth she was doing was giving me a fucking headache.

"I can't believe ya'll would kill him like that. What the fuck am I going to do now?" Trixie cried and we all just stood and looked at her like she was crazy.

"Give me one reason why you did all of this. What have we ever done to you? After all these years, you show up and try to hurt us and our family. That nigga didn't give a fuck about you. How could you choose him over us? Nasir said on the verge of tears. I knew this shit hurt him to the core. He missed our mother. She was his pick when we were younger. When she left, he used to sit on the porch and wait for her to come back.

"Ya'll ruined my life. I curse the day I birthed ya'll black asses." She said that shit with so much hatred in her voice. I really had to get this bitch out of my sight.

"Get the fuck up and get your ass out of here. If you value your fucking life, you will leave this city and never look back."

I untied her and yanked her up by the collar. I pushed her towards the exit and walked away. Gunshots caused me to stop in my tracks and looked back. Trixie was lying on the floor. Nasir was standing over her with a smoking gun. The tears that streamed from his eyes let me know it hurt him to do it. I took the gun out of his hands and pulled him into my arms. No matter how old Nasir gets, I will always and forever be my brother's keeper.

Epilogue- Gucci

It felt so good dancing with my husband for our first dance as husband and wife. *Forever More* by R. Kelly played in the background. I loved that song because it reminded me so much of us. I couldn't believe I was Mrs. King Montez Carter. I looked over at Chanel and Nasir dancing for the first time as husband and wife. My baby sister was officially Mrs. Nasir Montel Carter. Dior and Dutch were also dancing on the dance floor. Dior refused to marry him after all the bullshit with Natavia. Right now, they're just working on their relationship and starting over fresh.

I was proud of Dior. She was finding her happy and doing things her way. Dutch was hurt that she turned down his proposal and gave him the ring back. However, he knew it was his fuck-ups that made her question his love for her. It was all good though. Her ass got pregnant the night she got out of jail and let him fuck her. Hopefully, everything will fall into place for them.

My baby was looking good as hell in his all white tux. My pussy was wet as hell as he whispered sweet nothings in my ear. I looked over at KJ and Imani as they danced on the floor. Not long after the whole crew was up dancing off of throwback house music. I was surprised to see Thug dancing with Tahari. Everybody was having so much fun.

"I love you, Mrs. Carter."

"I love you more, Mr. Carter." We kissed each other with so much passion and held on to each other so tight. The moment of pure bliss ended when uninvited guests barged inside the reception hall. We were surrounded by Chicago's finest.

"King Carter, you're under arrest for running an illegal drug operation."

I cried as the officer placed handcuffs on him.

"Please don't do this. It's our wedding day."

Tears were falling down my face. KJ and Imani were crying as well.

"Stop crying, G. I'll be out sooner than you think. Hold shit down for me, Ma. I promise I'm coming home to you."

"Yeah, in about twenty fucking years." The officer said with a smirk on his face.

That shit caused me to cry even harder. I was so focused on King being led away in handcuffs I didn't notice that Nasir, Dutch, Malik, Sarge, Dro, and Quaadir were all in handcuffs and being led out as well.

"So, we meet again, Mr. Kenneth. I told you I was going to put you away for a long time," Detective Jones said as he took his handcuffs out of his back pocket. "Ka'Jaire Kenneth, you're under arrest for interstate drug trafficking and operating a criminal enterprise." The officer smirked as he placed the handcuffs on Thug.

"I love you, Boss Lady. Hold it down for me, Bonnie," Thug said to Tahari who was also crying.

They were staring in each other's eyes like they were telling each other something without actually saying words. Thug blew Tahari a kiss and then he was led away. All of the kids were crying uncontrollably. I couldn't believe this shit was happening on my fucking wedding day.

Chanel, Dior, Barbie, Ta'Jay, Keesha, and Khia were also crying as they tried to comfort their children who had just witnessed their fathers being led out in handcuffs. Tahari was no longer crying. She was standing there looking she wanted to kill somebody.

"Wipe your fucking faces right now. I know ya'll hurt but crying won't help us or them," Tahari said as she stood in front of all of us

"What are we going to do now?"

"We're going to keep this motherfucking business up and running. As of right now, I'm the head of this fucking family. Each one of you will run your nigga's territory until they come home. Make this the last time I see you crying. I don't want that weak shit on my team. I need all hands on deck to keep Thug Inc. up and running. Let's get the fuck out of here. Meet me at my house. There is money to be made and we never disappoint our clientele. Strap the fuck up, ladies. It's about be a bumpy ass ride."

Tahari turned on her heels and left the reception hall with all seven of her children in tow.

To Be Continued: Thug Paradise II Coming Soon

Made in the USA
Monee, IL
10 June 2022

97818682R00085